At War with the Mafia

"These people are not criminals in the usual sense," he once wrote in his journal. "They are a competitive power, a foreign nation within the nation, at war with everything our nation stands for, and yet protected by the very guarantees which they would deny us. It makes no sense to war upon a hostile foreign power while extending to them all the genteel courtesies which we reserve for ourselves. They mean to dominate us, to take away all our protections of law—they mean to conquer, to rape, and to loot this nation.

The only sensible response is to fight back—to destroy them if we can, when we can, as many as we can, and let the devil take the body-count. I am at war with an enemy of my country. And I intend to bring that enemy to its knees ... if I can."

THE EXECUTIONER SERIES:

#1   WAR AGAINST THE MAFIA
#2   DEATH SQUAD
#3   BATTLE MASK
#4   MIAMI MASSACRE
#5   CONTINENTAL CONTRACT
#6   ASSAULT ON SOHO
#7   NIGHTMARE IN NEW YORK
#8   CHICAGO WIPEOUT
#9   VEGAS VENDETTA
#10   CARIBBEAN KILL
#11   CALIFORNIA HIT
#12   BOSTON BLITZ
#13   WASHINGTON I.O.U.
#14   SAN DIEGO SIEGE
#15   PANIC IN PHILLY
#16   SICILIAN SLAUGHTER
#17   JERSEY GUNS
#18   TEXAS STORM
#19   DETROIT DEATHWATCH
#20   NEW ORLEANS KNOCKOUT
#21   FIREBASE SEATTLE
#22   HAWAIIAN HELLGROUND
#23   ST. LOUIS SHOWDOWN
#24   CANADIAN CRISIS
#25   COLORADO KILL-ZONE
#26   ACAPULCO RAMPAGE
#27   DIXIE CONVOY
#28   SAVAGE FIRE
#29   COMMAND STRIKE
#30   CLEVELAND PIPELINE
#31   ARIZONA AMBUSH
#32   TENNESSEE SMASH
#33   MONDAY'S MOB
#34   TERRIBLE TUESDAY
#35   WEDNESDAY'S WRATH
#36   THERMAL THURSDAY

the EXECUTIONER #36

THERMAL THURSDAY

by Don Pendleton

PINNACLE BOOKS   LOS ANGELES

EXECUTIONER #36: THERMAL THURSDAY

Copyright © 1979 by Don Pendleton

An original Pinnacle Books edition, published for the first time anywhere.

First printing, August 1979
Second printing, September 1979

ISBN: 0-523-40772-6

Cover illustration by Gil Cohen

Printed in the United States of America

PINNACLE BOOKS, INC.
2029 Century Park East
Los Angeles, California 90067

For Cecil Miles Buffalo,
a true warrior and a real man.

Let not young souls
  be smothered out
before they do quaint deeds
  and fully flaunt their pride.
—Vachel Lindsay (*The Congo*)

And the measure of our torment
  is the measure of our youth.
God help us,
  for we knew the worst too young!
—Rudyard Kipling (*Gentlemen Rankers*)

To know the truth is to be
responsible for it. God help me.
I knew too much, too young.
—Mack Bolan

THERMAL THURSDAY

PROLOGUE

What had begun as a simple and direct reaction to an unbearable situation had quickly escalated into the hottest and widest conflict to be waged within the American nation since the War Between the States: Mack Bolan's personal war against the Mafia.

Bolan had been an infantry sergeant in Vietnam, a highly trained career soldier with twelve years of service and several combat tours behind him, when his homefront war exploded upon the public awareness. It was an illegal war, of course, conducted without benefit of any official blessing, so Bolan himself was immediately

1

branded a criminal and quickly became the most sought-after fugitive in the country.

Not only the police wanted Mack Bolan's body; the Mafia, too, "the enemy," reacting in typical fashion, at first issued an almost casual "open contract" on the life of this impertinent challenger, a reaction which itself escalated in direct proportion to the challenge. Within a very short time, the response to "the Bolan problem" became a nationwide effort of unmatched proportions, with both the cops and the killers determinedly shrinking that fragile zone between them, which Bolan called "no man's land."

The brilliant military tactician played that zone for all it was worth, though, and succeeded in mounting and maintaining a progression of dramatic and effective guerrilla campaigns against "this all-pervading enemy, the invisible second government of the United States." Bolan would not, however, take on the official government. He would not fire upon a law officer, nor would he respond with force of any kind to the police effort. This left him a single alternative: he simply had to avoid all contact with police authority. That was not always possible, of course, even though it was common knowledge that many police officers were secretly sympathetic to the Bolan crusade and were themselves avoiding a confrontation.

On those few occasions when the confrontation was unavoidable, it seemed that the redoubtable sergeant from Vietnam always walked away with a new friend and his freedom intact. There was something about the man that inspired confidence and admiration—a personal quality which could be defined only as "high character"—an aura of ethics and competence to which only the worst of men could not respond favorably.

Some called it "the Bolan effect."

Harold Brognola called it "human excellence." Brognola headed a federally organized crime strike force at the time of his first encounter with Bolan, early in the war. Thanks in large part to the symbiotic relationship which then grew between the two, Brognola advanced rapidly to the number two position in the U.S. Justice Department and advisor to the president. Bolan also benefited from the exchange of intelligence, which began to "possibilize the impossible."

There had never been a moment, in the beginning, when Sergeant Bolan dared dream that he could actually succeed in his self-appointed task to rid the country of the Mafia presence. How could a lone man hope to succeed where armies of cops and the legal might of the greatest nation on earth had failed? Yet it was just that failure of the official system that had prompted Bolan to action. He had never hoped to go the full route. In his own understanding, he had consigned his fate to that of "the condemned man's last mile." And his chief aim was to make it a very bloody last mile indeed, to take as many of the enemy to hell with him as he could possibly manage.

As the war blazed on, Bolan himself could not point to any certain moment where the impossible had become possibilized. His entire life had become a constant walk through hell without letup, without rest, without even pause. He slept with his eyes open, ate on the run, and counted every heartbeat as though it would be his last. There was nothing romantic or even remotely enviable about the life he had chosen for himself. And though he freely looted the enemy's illicit treasures, all the money thus liberated was plowed directly back into the war effort; Bolan had no Swiss bank accounts or Wall Street portfolios. He lived a life of simple immediacy and pointed significance: he lived only to eradicate the Mafia. Nor could he be content with seeing the enemy behind bars. He knew too well the many crime kingdoms flourishing from behind the temporary inconvenience of prison bars, of the seeming inability of the American justice system to deal with the spreading cancer of organized crime.

"These people are not criminals in the usual sense," he once wrote in his journal. "They are a competitive power, a foreign nation within the nation, at war with everything our nation stands for, and yet protected by the very guarantees which they would deny us. It makes no sense to war upon a hostile foreign power while extending to them all the genteel courtesies which

4

we reserve for ourselves. They mean to dominate us, to take away all our protections of law—they mean to conquer, to rape, and to loot this nation. The only sensible response is to fight back—to destroy them if we can, when we can, as many as we can, and let the devil take the bodycount. I am at war with an enemy of my country. And I intend to bring that enemy to its knees . . . if I can."

But he never actually thought that he could.

It was Hal Brognola who first suggested that the impossible had become possible for Mack Bolan. In Brognola's view, Bolan's thirty-odd campaigns against the underworld power centers had greatly weakened their all-important infrastructure and had decimated the leadership to a point where a long-frustrated legal system was, for the first time ever, beginning to gain some real control over the problem of organized crime in America. He wanted Bolan to step down, to end that war—and to begin another of far greater importance (in Brognola's view), but this time under full governmental recognition and support.

The new problem was the threat and spread of international terrorism, to which a concerned nation was groping for effective countermeasures. What better man than Mack Bolan to head up a new counter-terrorist force to deal with the problem? With the job would come full forgiveness of all past illegal acts, a cover identity, and official status within the government.

While Bolan recognized the urgency of the new national concern, he did not share completely Brognola's assessment of the underworld situation. It was very difficult for this man to turn away from a commitment so diligently pursued through so much hell. He considered the government's request, then told Brognola: "Okay. I accept. But first . . ."

But first the guy wanted to do it all over again.

Brognola reported to the president: "He's in, sir. But he insists on delaying a week. He feels he has to do a second mile."

"A second what?" asked the man in the oval office.

"You know, like in the Bible. If a man asks you to walk a mile with him . . ."

"Go with him twain," sighed the president.

"Something like that—yes, sir. He didn't put it just that way. But he does want to mount a six-day mop-up of the remaining trouble centers."

"Give him all covert support possible," was the final response by the president. "But get him here, Hal—get the man here, alive and well, one week from today."

So began Mack Bolan's second bloody mile, a highly compressed timetable for final victory. The impossible had become possibilized. Not assured. Only possibilized. These final six days would tell the tale. If he could survive them while accomplishing the prime objectives . . .

6

well, yeah, he could then turn away with a clean conscience.

But there had been too much bloodshed, too many agonies of mind and body, the price altogether too high along that first savage mile to even contemplate an empty peace. Mack Bolan would turn away from nothing short of a real and meaningful victory.

The first three days had gone okay . . . okay enough. But they had raised grave doubts in the mind of the man who, in the beginning, had promised himself that he would "shake their house down." The impossible had become *possible* . . . that was all.

But now it was the fourth day. The place was Florida. The time was Thursday. The situation was, yeah, possible . . . but just barely.

1

H-HOUR

It was a dawn landing, with nothing but a makeshift windsock emplaced beside the dirt strip to guide the way in. Grimaldi made a sign with his thumb and went around one time at low altitude for a quick recon. Bolan checked the action on his Beretta then returned the piece to concealment beneath a Levi's jacket as he scanned the layout below.

The hammock was several hundred yards long by maybe a hundred wide, barely distinguishable from the sea of sawgrass marshland surrounding it. There were no trees and hardly any vegetation—an indication that someone had farmed the tiny island in recent times. Now it was little more than a primitive airstrip buried deep within the Florida Everglades, one of those countless oases-in-reverse that dot the shallow waters. There were no manmade structures on this one except for a rickety pier near the north end of the airstrip. A couple of small boats were alongside and a swamp buggy had been run ashore close by.

Bolan counted five human figures standing in a clump at the north end of the strip. Off to the west about a mile, two large swamp buggies were approaching the hammock via a narrow channel of open water imbedded in tall grass; that presence would be undetectable from the surface of the hammock.

"I guess it's going down," Bolan muttered to his pilot.

"They said dawn," Grimaldi grunted. "Is it a go?"

"Yeah, go," Bolan replied without emotion.

They went, a wing of the twin Cessna dipping into a ninety-degree turn as Grimaldi lined up with the runway.

The thing was going down, and Bolan was not thinking of the descent of the airplane. "It" was going down—no question about it. Death was overhanging that tranquil scene below—a heavy, smothering presence which a man such as Mack Bolan had long ago learned to recognize as an entity—to be felt on the skin like hot wind, tasted on the lips like brine—entering the body like smoke through the lungs to energize the bloodstream with quiet whisperings.

Death was here, yes—palpable, imminent, unavoidable.

Bolan and his partner could avoid it, though—this time, this place. Those down below could not; and, of course, it was Bolan's task to challenge, not to evade.

"See the devil force?" the pilot inquired quietly as he continued the landing procedure.

"About a mile west," Bolan replied.

"Yeah—I thought I caught a glimpse. Okay. Here we go. This could be a rough one. Grab your teeth."

But it was not so rough a landing. The heavily mineraled soil of the hammock was nicely compacted and relatively smooth for a dirt strip. The Cessna used only about a third of the available runway for the landing roll then turned about for a quick return to the offload area at the north end, where the reception party waited.

Some party. They were mere kids, those five. And two of them were female.

Grimaldi ground his teeth as he commented, "Would you look at that! Babes in joyland! What the hell do they think they're . . . ?"

"Kids younger than that died in Nam," Bolan growled.

"Sure, but . . . two of these are baby *dolls*!"

"Equal rights," Bolan muttered and stepped outside.

Baby dolls, right. Pert, smiling, overly energized by the thrill of the adventure—dancing eyes, butts wiggling in too-tight jeans as they strode forward in greeting.

Baby guys, too. Not your stereotype smuggler, for sure. These guys would look more natural at a pantyraid or pep rally. Bright . . . aware . . . alive. Nothing really terminal could ever happen to them, could it? Life was just a game, wasn't it, after all? The worst that could happen was that you would not collect your two hundred dollars as you passed "Go." Right?

Wrong.

Bolan showed those bright smiling faces his Beretta as he coldly commanded, "Get in the plane. No arguments. Just do it."

Bright smiles turned to worried frowns and questioning glances furtively exchanged, but all five entered the Cessna, doing it with no arguments and no vocal comments whatever.

They probably thought it was a bust. Big deal. So they would not collect their two hundred bucks: Go to jail; go straight to jail; do not collect your two hundred dollars.

Grimaldi kicked a couple of bundles to the ground as he said something quick and quiet to his new passengers, then he quickly spun the plane around and returned aloft.

The two bundles appeared to be identical. One, however, contained hi-grade cocaine worth well beyond two hundred bucks, for sure, in the underground trade. The other contained a wicked little Uzi submachine gun, some extra

11

ammo clips, and two fragmentation grenades.

Bolan carried the bundles to the pier and was opening the one containing the weapons when a miniature breast-pocket radio beeped an incoming signal. He extended the antenna and responded, "Striker."

Grimaldi's voice came back immediately with a terse report from high overhead. "Two hundred yards off the pier in high grass and moving in. It's a double. I count four per each."

Two buggies, eight guns . . . the "devil force." It was a new phrase being whispered about the 'glades and along the Florida coasts, a new version of a very old game . . . modern pirates preying upon the smuggling lanes with a savagery never approached by Blackbeard. But this bunch was not going to find unarmed college kids awaiting their mercy. Instead, this time, they were going to find . . .

Bolan replied, "Okay. Keep it cool. Eyes open."

"Betcher ass," was the response.

Bolan smiled solemnly as he tucked the radio away. Grimaldi had been a good friend and able ally throughout much of the war. The guy was a mob pilot. Once, down in Puerto Rico, he'd done his best to do Bolan in. And vice versa. But one of those strange twists of fate made friends of natural enemies and added an important new dimension to Bolan's war effort. The guy could fly anything with wings. And, as it turned out, he had no particular love for his employers. Besides becoming a valuable intelligence source, Grimaldi also had combat experience and was a capable and reliable soldier in the hotspots. It was Grimaldi's contacts that had led Bolan into the new game in Florida—and that game involved quite a bit more than simple pirating. This was a mere starting point.

And it started like so many others.

Out of the grass suddenly appeared the snakes. One man in each boat carried an automatic weapon. The other guys packed pistols in side leather. They'd done this before . . . many times. It was sheer routine now. They even looked bored. The buggies were twenty yards out and proceeding abreast when a guy picked up a bullhorn and called ahead, "Just cool it, mister. Don't move, don't even breathe hard, and you'll be okay."

Bolan was cool, he wasn't breathing hard, and he felt quite okay. Both hands were inside the weapons cache, wherein a grenade with a ten second fuse was receiving its prime. At ten yards out, he produced the little bomb and tossed it with an underhand flip toward the approaching raiding party.

The startled reaction could have been produced by something as harmless as an apple or an orange; it was like one of those surprise encounters along the Ho Chi Minh Trail where the instinctive reaction precedes rational thought and everyone involved follows his own spontaneous sparking of the survival pattern.

13

A couple of guys hit the water; others flung themselves to the decks in a scramble for protection; one of the burpers cut loose with a wild burst into the air—and all this before the fuse found its ten-count.

Bolan was in the shallow water beside the pier, Uzi in hand and bracketing the target zone, when the grenade exploded. It had found its mark in the air about ten feet above the buggies. One of them lurched away in a quick turn with no one aboard then came about and ran aground a few yards downrange. The other was ablaze and foundering almost instantly, a dead man at the controls. A scared-looking guy with a sub-machine gun stood in waist-deep water and gawked at the carnage about him. Bolan cut that guy diagonally across the chest with a burst from the Uzi, then sent another chasing a couple of swimmers who were threshing toward the tall grass.

That left a single survivor, a guy with a bleeding pattern spreading across his backside, who was painfully pulling himself aboard the beached swamp buggy.

Bolan deliberately failed to see that guy, instead sending concentrated fire into the burning craft until it exploded and sent its parts hurtling across the disturbed waters. When next he looked, the other buggy was creeping into the sawgrass and disappearing from view some fifty yards downstream.

Good enough.

14

He activated his radio and sent the report aloft: "Okay down here. The rest is yours."

"Have him in sight," came the response. "Just call me flypaper."

Bolan smiled grimly and pocketed the radio. He gathered his stuff and fired up the buggy that had been brought there by the kids, took a last look around, then put that place behind him.

It seemed a strange place for a beginning . . . but perfectly fitting as an end to a particular devil force. How many hammocks had they left this way—with how many unarmed amateurs left as a picnic spread for the 'gators?

Too many, if only one.

But this was Thursday morning—and a modest beginning for a day which would have to see a vicious crime empire dismantled and flung into the muck.

Thursday, yeah . . . hot Thursday . . . *thermal* Thursday. And so the day began.

2

TRULY ALIVE

Harold Brognola had been in charge of the official U.S. government response to organized crime since shortly after Mack Bolan began his own unofficial war on the mob. The two men had been covert allies through much of the Bolan experience, exchanging intelligence and sometimes joining forces in joint operations against a common threat—but the chief fed had never been completely comfortable with his secret liaisons with a man who was also, at the same moment, prominent on the FBI's most-wanted list. It was a question of not only official ethics but of personal principles, as well. Brognola was a man of strong moral fiber. The association with Bolan was therefore a troubling one, creating inner conflicts which sometimes approached crisis proportions.

Once, in fact, Brognola had actually pulled the trigger on this man whom he admired and respected—whom, indeed, he loved like a brother. That the trigger pull did not result in Mack Bolan's death was nothing to the credit or debit (however you chose to look at it) of Hal Brognola. Fate, or whatever, had intervened—and the remarkable outcome of all that was the incredible fact that Bolan understood and forgave, as though it had never happened. Not so incredible, though, when you really knew the man.

For all of Brognola's moral and ethical strength, he knew that Mack Bolan was far more the ideal man than Brognola himself would ever be. The guy was one of those flaming anachronisms, born far beyond his time, capable of a degree of personal commitment and dedication unmatched in modern men.

Nor was the guy all blood and ice, either.

In the words of a former Vietnam buddy, "The Sarge is a man who can carry both heart and guts in the same body at the same time." Indeed —though Bolan had first earned his Executioner tag in the hellgrounds of Vietnam, he had also become quietly known among the medics there as Sergeant Mercy.

Said one surgeon at a forward medical facility: "This man Bolan has singlehandedly done

17

more for the American cause in the unpacified areas than any official program I know of."

It seemed that the Executioner—whose missions as a penetration specialist routinely took him into hostile territories—routinely carried with him unofficial gifts of much-needed medical supplies for the civilian victims of that savage time.

"More often than not," the surgeon said, "he came back with a dying old man or woman strapped to his back and a kid under each arm. The man has incredible strength and perseverance. I know personally of one occasion when he carried a maimed child through more than twenty miles of enemy country while under hot pursuit by the enemy. Not only that, he doctored the kid along the way and kept her alive. At his own great peril, of course. And that was only one of many such occasions. It wasn't the medics who first began calling Bolan Sergeant Mercy. That's the literal translation of the name given him by the villagers. But that wasn't his job, you know. He's not a medic."

No, Sergeant Mercy was not a medic. The enemy soldiers and officials knew him by another name, which translates as the Executioner. And he is perhaps the only soldier in modern times to have a price placed on his head by an enemy command.

So . . . how to separate the pieces? Was Mack Bolan a cold and methodical killer or was he a courageous and compassionate champion of the human cause?

Brognola had found the threads of separation and—in so doing—had discovered that there was no separation of the pieces of Mack Bolan's character. The pieces all fit together into a coherent pattern to produce the total personality of a man who simply could not and would not turn away from his own vision of "right."

It was "right" that he kill certain individuals, only because he had become convinced that a higher and vital good was thereby being served. And, of course, that higher good was tied directly to his sense of compassion together with a willingness toward personal sacrifice.

Ipso facto, Mack Bolan was at war with the mob.

Also *ipso facto,* it was a total war utterly devoid of artificial restraints or personal reservations toward comfort and/or convenience.

Most importantly, though, Bolan's war was strongly discriminating and selective. It served no "good" whatever to sacrifice innocent victims in the pursuit of right. Unlike the terrorist mentality which killed and maimed indiscriminately in pursuit of a cause, Bolan's war took excruciating pains to separate the guilty from the innocent, to define the enemy and isolate him within the parameters of a secure war zone before the shooting began.

The guy had seen too much innocent suffering

in Southeast Asia. He did not intend to inflict that same pain on his own people, at home. This was, indeed, the very thing that he was fighting against.

So, no—Mack Bolan did not cruise Central Park tossing bombs at joggers as his response to crime in the streets. Nor was he a zealot who could justify any price paid for the success of his undertaking. Many times the guy had canceled a scheduled showdown or broke off in the midst of hostilities, at his own immense peril, because of innocent intruders into the scene.

Paradoxical or not, the guy was practically a saint: a saint with a gun in one hand and a grenade in the other—either of which he would drop instantly to extend that hand to an innocent in need.

A saint with bloody hands . . .

Perhaps that was overstating the case but for Hal Brognola it was not a severe overstatement. Still, there were those troubling moments when the chief fed felt like a man who was balancing precariously upon the edge of a sharp knife. Even now, with the White House itself committed to and covertly supporting the operation, Brognola was uneasy in his role as prime backstop for Mack Bolan's illegal war.

And Bolan understood all that, of course. Hell, the guy would be the first to send Brognola packing. He had, in fact, tried to do that very thing many times. And since the furious progression of events during this "second mile" effort,

Bolan's most persistently spoken words were "Get off my shadow, Hal."

But, hell, there was no way to get off the guy's shadow, now. Too much was at stake. It was not just Bolan's life—it wasn't just the elimination of a few pockets of organized crime. What was at stake, now, was a powderkeg international situation and very possibly the fate of a free America in a very restless and troubled world. A guy like Mack Bolan could spell a large difference in that equation. The man's entire lifetime had been shaping and preparing him for this moment in history, a moment when man and situation coincided for a destined role in the further development of the nation. You could take all the generals and all the cops and roll them together and still not come up with as good a solution as that one man, Mack Bolan, had to offer to the growing problem of terrorist intrigue.

So, yes, a lot was at stake.

Brognola's sole concern, now, was to deliver Mack Bolan whole and healthy to the man in the oval office at the conclusion of this second-mile stroll through hell. That could be a formidable task, especially when the guy in question kept growling, "Get off my shadow."

Complicating that situation was another individual who kept urging closer and closer involvement. That individual was presently pacing back and forth while glowering at a large wall chart of the Everglades region. And it helped not a whit that this individual was a subordinate in Brognola's own department.

Some individuals simply refuse to be subordinated.

Especially some female individuals.

Who also happen to be personally involved in a case. This one looked more like a *Glamour* model than a federal operative. And she was very deeply involved in the case at hand.

"Stop pacing, dammit," Brognola growled. "That isn't going to buy you a thing."

"I don't need a thing," April Rose growled back. "And I guess *he* doesn't, either. Why doesn't he report in?"

"Relax," said the chief fed. "It's only an hour past dawn. Give the guy some time, will you?"

"An hour is plenty time enough," she mused. "Have you ever been on the firing line with that man? Let me tell you, things happen very quickly when Striker is on the job."

Striker was, of course, Bolan. It was one of those little bureaucratic hypocrisies that he was never referred to by his own name during covert support. As though not mentioning the name somehow made it all nice and legal.

"You're right," Brognola said, allowing his own anxiety to surface for a moment. "We'll move on the area in thirty minutes, if there's been no word by then."

"What's wrong with right now?" April countered. She was a lovely girl—a tall, striking brunette with a body to make men's minds

22

wander—but she could also be irritatingly pushy, even from a subordinate position.

"Back off, April," Brognola gently commanded. "Don't let personal feelings color your judgment. You have to give the guy room to operate. And you'd better learn that damn quick, if you mean to have a personal role in his life."

"*What* life?" she replied miserably. "It's not a life. It's a sort of death."

True, too true.

But Bolan himself would have argued with that finding. "A man is not truly alive," said an early entry in his personal journal, "until he has found something worth dying for."

Brognola told the anxious young lady: "Then that's what you have to share with him, honey. A sort of death."

"He won't even share that with me," she sniffed.

The chief fed sighed and gave his worried subordinate a tender hug. "What Striker has right now is not fit for sharing, particularly not with someone he loves. Try to understand that, from his viewpoint. And try to remember that it's our job, yours and mine, to help him find something that *is* worth sharing."

"That's what I'm trying to do," the lady whispered.

"Then you help him first by understanding, and by respecting, and by giving him room. He knows what he's doing and he's damned good at what he does. But don't add to the natural jeopardy by hovering about and looking on. We simply can't do that."

"You're saying I just have to accept him as he is, on his own terms, even if it's over his own dead body."

"Yeah." Brognola turned away from those suffering eyes. "But it's only for a few more days. Give the guy that much."

And she would. She'd give the guy that much. But Brognola knew how difficult it could be. Hell . . . didn't he love the guy like a brother? And wouldn't he gladly share "a sort of death" with a man of Mack Bolan's caliber? More, sure, more than that . . . he'd share the grave itself.

Hal Brognola was something of a battle-line philosopher himself. And he had an understanding which was roughly equivalent to Bolan's. It went something like this: To be truly dead, a man has only to disinvolve himself from the higher goals of humanity

"We're moving," he announced suddenly, giving in to a gut decision.

"You mean right now?"

Yeah. He meant right now. A "sort of death" could be bad enough. To be "dead" was for sure a hard thing to contemplate. But to be among the "truly dead" was just downright intolerable.

3

THE GAMESMEN

The illicit drug trade was being called Florida's largest industry, and a harried police establishment was publicly admitting that less than 10 percent of the illegal substances were being intercepted through the combined efforts of federal, state, and local agencies. With an annual trade running into billions of dollars, a math degree was not required to calculate the risk statistics for an enterprising businessman. It was not surprising, then, that an ever-increasing number of amateurs were taking a fling at that market, amateurs from every economic and social sector.

But it was a statistic also quickly learned by

every savvy street kid—and some of those "kids" had gone on to graduate *magna cum laude* with degrees in professional crime. Such degrees were characteristically delivered with blood all over them, the bloodiest of all being awarded to the meanest of all competitors.

Bolan understood those statistics, too. And he knew that the risk factor for professionals was far more favorable than the one-in-ten factor for amateurs. For the organized professional, moreover, the risk factor was perhaps one chance in a hundred for being caught in the act—and the risk of actually going to jail was probably 10 percent of that.

So it was a very lucrative field of endeavor for the professional criminal, and this fact would inevitably give rise to another factor. Given a thousand-to-one shot for illicit profits on a grand scale, Bolan knew from past experience that the meanest of all would be moving very determinedly to take it all over.

All of which, of course, would increase by quantum leaps the risk factor for the amateur entrepeneur, the loser paying with his own blood.

And, lately, there had been many such losers.

The grim truth of the matter was that the mob made better cops than the cops. They knew all the angles and avenues, all the sources and middlemen, and they would not hesitate to apply money and force in their domination of the trade lanes.

But some smart operator had apparently discovered an even better game. Really, it was not much different from the hijack game of the Prohibition era, in which many mobsters made fortunes by cashing in other men's investments. The new Florida game apparently worked much the same way. Let the kids and other amateurs make their buys and smuggle the stuff into the country—thereby assuming most of the risks—then the smart operator would simply knock them over and take the stuff for himself. It was even possible that the source or middleman who sold the stuff in Colombia or wherever was under the control of the same man or men who controlled the hijackers.

It was a neat game, yeah.

Bolan knew that it was something along this line that had been worked in the present situation. For sure, Grimaldi's source knew where the buy had gone down, knew how it was being transported, and knew where it was to be received in the U.S. The guy had the whole timetable. The mob could have made their hit at any point along the way. Playing the percentages, though, the hit would come only after the product had safely entered the country.

Grimaldi had pre-empted that schedule, making his own "hit" at an intermediate point—which is how Mack Bolan happened to be playing delivery man in that dawn drop—and which is why five dispirited young people were far better off than they probably realized.

27

They sat in the dirt just inside the small hangar, sipping beer from cans and conversing in hushed tones. The conversation froze and all eyes turned his way as Bolan stepped inside. He gave a curt nod and strode past the group without a word.

He found Grimaldi at a rickety desk in the office of the temporary base camp, bent over an aeronautical sectional chart and busily applying pencil and protractor to a small problem in navigation. The pilot looked up with a grin and reported, "I think we struck some paydirt."

"How much?" Bolan inquired quietly.

"Maybe a whole yard." Grimaldi fingered a penciled circle on the chart as he explained, "The guy beat it straight to this hammock, here. It's maybe a thousand yards in diameter, maybe a bit more. It's inhabited. I counted two large buildings and maybe half a dozen smaller ones, grouped around a small lagoon on the west side. Or maybe that lagoon is a large pond. I couldn't really get a good angle on it without becoming too obvious. Either it's a lagoon or a pond sitting right at the edge of the land area."

Bolan eyed the map as he asked, "What's that big island just to the north?"

"That one's the kicker," the pilot replied, grinning broadly. "Remember I told you about Tommy Santelli's sugar cane investment?"

"Uh huh."

"That big island just to the north is Tommy's farm. I flew some guys in there a few months ago, right after they took it over. How much you want to bet he owns the lagoon hammock, too? You could damn near swim from one to the other. Or wade it. Course, I wouldn't want to do either. That's 'gator country. And snakes. God knows what else."

"You're sure the guy went to the small island?"

"No doubt about it. He was hurting. I saw two guys carrying him toward the buildings."

"Any chance you were spotted?"

"Not much. I played the sun all I could. For sure the dude in the boat didn't spot me. From the way he was handling that swamp buggy, I'd say he wasn't seeing much of anything. The guy just barely made it, Sarge. We got damned lucky on that one."

"The kids tumble to what you were doing?"

"I doubt that. I think they were all in a state of shock, most of that flight."

"Give you any trouble?"

Grimaldi smiled. "Not really. Watch the tall blonde, though. She tried to vamp me."

Bolan returned the smile. "But you were strong."

"As a rock. They're okay kids. Sort of confused, right now, and wondering what the hell. I gave them a six-pack and told them to cool it." He spread his hands. "What can they do?"

"They can thank heaven for large favors," Bolan muttered.

"They know that. They saw. That's why the shock."

"You tell them anything, yet?"

"Naw. That's your department."

Bolan sighed and lit a cigarette then stared at the chart for a moment. Finally he said, "I guess we need to update Alice. Will you take care of that for me?"

Alice was Hal Brognola, waiting somewhere in the wings with a hot-hot force of federal marshals, poised to strike upon signal.

Grimaldi replied, "Sure. Just an update?"

"That's all."

"You don't want to talk to him?"

"Not yet, no," Bolan replied quietly. There was a bit of strain in the relationship at the moment, due entirely to Bolan's own misgivings about the future being charted for him by Brognola and others in Washington. And, no, he was not yet ready to talk to his old friend from the Wonderland by the Potomac.

"I'll just, uh, report the developments," said Grimaldi. "And tell him to hang loose."

"Very loose, yeah," Boland agreed, and went out for a parley with the kids.

They were obviously ready to parley. All scrambled to their feet at his approach and showed him expectant, tense faces. He asked, quietly, "Everyone okay?"

It was not what they had expected to hear; the question threw them, momentarily. The tall blonde girl was the first to respond vocally. She said, small voiced, "We're okay, sure. We'd just like to know what's going on."

A lanky boy beside her added, "Are we under arrest, or what? And what about Luke?"

"Luke" was the sixth partner in the enterprise.

Bolan quietly informed them, "Luke's okay. He's in Key West. And no one is under arrest. I'm not a cop."

"Then what are you?" asked the blonde.

Bolan ignored that question to ask one of his own. "Which one of you is David Johnson?"

The lanky one shifted his feet and raised a hand to about shoulder level.

Bolan opened his shirt and produced a packet of cash which he handed over to the youth. "That covers your investment in the product," he told him.

The kid looked stunned. "What . . . wh . . . ?" he stammered.

"I'm buying you out," Bolan explained.

The others were a bit mind-blown, too. The blonde girl said something unintelligibly exclamatory but she was the only one with a vocal response.

Bolan told them one and all: "You're out your expenses. I won't cover that. But count your blessings. You got out cheap. If you try it again then you're plain stupid. Now go home, beat it. You'll find your boat on the west shore."

He turned his back on them and returned to the office. When he turned back from the doorway, all were gone . . . almost. The tall blonde girl had followed him. He looked at her closely for the first time, realizing only then that she

31

was a bit different from the others. A bit older, for one thing. Much more deeply tanned, for another—the mark, perhaps, of one who'd been in sunny Florida much longer than a casual visitor.

Bolan growled at her, "I told you to beat it."

"Nuts to that," she replied evenly. "I want to know what your game is. Are you a federal narc?"

"Are you?" Bolan countered.

She smiled and shook her head. "I'm just a gal looking for a game."

"You wouldn't like this one," Bolan assured her.

"I've liked it great, so far," she replied spritely.

"Then you're insane," he said.

The girl kept right on smiling as she responded to that. "Maybe. And maybe I just like my men big, strong, brave, and slightly insane."

"Save it," he said harshly. "If you don't want to be stranded on this clot of dirt then you'd better hurry and catch your friends."

But she wasn't giving it up . . . and apparently she knew what she was about. "You're Mack Bolan, aren't you," she asked, though it really was not a question.

"Who?"

"Who, hell," said the blonde, blithely, as she moved past him and into the office.

And it seemed, yeah, that "the game" had suddenly grown more complex.

4

HANDLES

Her name, she said, was Jean Russell. But she could not produce identification to verify that and her story was not particularly convincing. The lady claimed that she had met David Johnson at a house party in Fort Lauderdale just one week earlier and that she had accompanied the group into the 'glades "just for kicks."

Grimaldi, who was just concluding his contact with the federal force when the girl entered the office, was greatly irritated by her presence in there. He did not like the way she was eyeing his aeronautical chart nor, obviously, did he like much of anything about the lady. He folded the chart and put it away, telling Bolan, "She stinks."

The girl smiled tolerantly at the open insult and said to Grimaldi, "I've been in the swamp all night without my Dial. What's your excuse?"

"It's not your body that stinks, honey," the pilot growled.

She flashed brilliant blue eyes at Bolan and said, "Well thank God for that. What's your verdict, Strong and Silent?"

Bolan showed her a tight grin as he replied to that. "Same as my partner's. But it really doesn't matter. We will be leaving in a few minutes. So there's no need to form friendships, is there?"

"You wouldn't leave me out here," she said soberly.

"No," Bolan agreed. "We wouldn't. We'll take you back to civilization. Then we say goodbye."

"Oh, nuts," the lady said with a sigh, lowering her well rounded backside onto the desk and slumping forward dejectedly.

"Never should've said hello," the pilot growled, though his voice softening just a bit.

"You're right about that, good-looking," she said. "You've been right all along. I do stink. Whoever said I could make it as an actress, anyway."

"What's the name of the act?" Bolan inquired softly.

"Jean Kirkpatrick, songs and dances. But I'm not acting, now. And you don't remember me, do you."

The name brushed the tendril of an old memory cell in the Bolan brain but nothing was focusing. He replied, "Surely I would. If we'd met."

"If we'd met," the girl echoed, smiling wistfully at Jack Grimaldi. "The man saved my life. Then turned it completely around." The gaze skipped back to Bolan. "I don't mean today . . . this time around. I mean . . . you're supposed to have a photographic memory. I've been keeping a scrapbook on you, ever since that—well, no, that isn't fair. I don't look the same. I wasn't a blonde." She bent her head and quickly popped a blue-tinted contact lens into her palm. "I don't even feel the same. And it has been a long time."

Bolan's gaze was dissecting the lady, now, taking her apart and reconstructing the features with different hair, different clothing, different . . .

The tendril flared suddenly, igniting an entire bank of submerged memories.

"Johnny Portocci," Bolan said quietly.

"Right," she said, smiling and stretching the word into several syllables. "And later you came to see me."

"Palmetto Lane, Miami."

She flashed a triumphant glance toward Grimaldi. "He *does* have a photographic memory."

"Why didn't you tell me straight off?" Bolan inquired. "Why the game?"

35

"Well, I . . ." The eyes fell to an inspection of her hands. "In the first place, I *have* been playing a game—ever since you left your mark on Miami—and on me, too. The police helped me establish a new identity, a new life. My legal name really is Russell, now. But I wasn't testing your memory, not really. I was hoping to beat it."

"Why?"

She clasped her hands and rocked around a bit on the desk before responding. "I was afraid you'd think I was still—you know—I was still working for them."

"What's she talking about?" Grimaldi asked quietly.

"It's okay to tell him," the girl said, still looking at her hands.

Bolan said to his partner, "It was early in the war, Jack. Before you, even. Miami was the fourth campaign."

"Sure, I know," said Grimaldi. "Everyone in the outfit heard about that one. But I was there, myself. I flew Ciro Lavangetta to that meet. But he flew out in a pine box. Him and a bunch of other bosses. But where was *she* in all that?"

Bolan said, "She was one of Vin Balderone's party girls for that meet."

Grimaldi made an "O" with his lips. He retreated to a chair at the back wall and dropped into it, removing himself from the reunion.

Bolan asked the lady, "So what are you doing out here in the 'glades?"

"I told you I had a new life," she replied soberly.

"Don't tell me you're a narc."

"That's pretty close."

"How close?"

"I take assignments from a couple of state narcotics officers. Not, uh, I'm not a cop. I work with undercover officers, sometimes, when they need cover reinforcement."

"For pay?"

"Sure, for pay. What else?"

"How'd you get into that?"

She sighed and rubbed an eye then reinserted the contact lens. "It's clear glass," she explained. "I mean, there's no vision correction. Purely cosmetic."

"How'd you get into that?" Bolan repeated.

She sighed again. "Remember the detective who got shot up that night, outside my house?"

"Wilson," Bolan recalled.

"Right. I visited him in the hospital a couple of times. We became friends. One thing led to another. I met these other friends of his. Things kept leading on. Incidentally, Bob Wilson is strongly aware that he owes you his life. And he's keeping a scrapbook, too."

"Who were you covering for, this morning?"

She said, "Can I have a cigarette?"

Bolan gave her one and held the light for her. She took a deep pull and made an unhappy face as she exhaled the smoke. "These damn things will kill you, Mack," she said softly.

"I'll worry about it," he replied, matching her tone.

"See what you mean," she said, glancing about the drab surroundings. "You do have a grim life, don't you."

"Why aren't you answering my question?" he asked her.

"I'm thinking about it."

"Or thinking something up?"

She gave a sober little giggle and replied, "No, I'm through trying to game you. It's just that it's sort of involved and . . . well, I do have certain obligations. You can understand that."

He said, "Sure, I can understand that. And you can understand, I'm sure, why I'll be dropping you at the first airport."

"But I can help you," she said quietly.

"Help me do what?"

"Bust the pirates. Isn't that the game?"

Bolan stared at the lady for a moment before replying, "That's part of it. But I'm not overly interested in burning ants. I want the hill."

"That's what I figured," she said soberly. "And that's why I want a piece of the action."

"You said you're not a cop."

"Right."

"And this has nothing to do with cover."

"That's right. This one is personal."

"But you can't say why."

"No, I really can't. Not yet."

Bolan said, "Stay." He jerked his eyes at Grimaldi and stepped outside the office.

38

The pilot followed him into the hangar. "Are you buying that?" Grimaldi muttered in a troubled voice.

"Did you talk to Brognola?"

"Not personally. But I filed the report. I get the idea they're moving up."

"Dammit!" Bolan quietly exclaimed.

"Are you buying this chick?"

Bolan sighed and said, "I'm willing to play the face value. How about you?"

"I still don't like the smell," Grimaldi replied. "But you're the man. I guess if we play it cool . . . we do have a ways to go. And your timetable doesn't allow much time for shadow boxing. So it's your decision. But, Sarge, you know— a lot of guys still have a hell of a hard-on for you. If that honeypot *is* still tied to the boys . . . well, need I say, she could write her own ticket anywhere in the world with your blood. How do you know she hasn't been spotting for the devil forces? I mean, lay it out, that would be the logical way to explain her involvement with those kids."

"It would," Bolan agreed. "But what you said about shadow boxing is also very true. We need a handle, Jack—a firm handle. Lay it out another way: true or false, friend or enemy, this girl could be that handle."

"It's a hell of a dangerous game," the pilot nervously pointed out. "But if you have a gut feeling . . ."

"I don't," Bolan told him. "That's the problem.

The guts are telling me nothing. I guess I just have to take it and run with it. But this could affect you, too. You rate a vote in the matter."

"I quit voting long ago," the pilot said with a wry grin. "In Puerto Rico. I've been keeping a scrapbook, too, guy. Besides, all I do is drive. You're the man."

Bolan smiled and gripped his friend's shoulder as he told him, "Get ready to drive, then. I'll go collect the baggage."

"Are we hitting Santelli's hammock?"

"Not yet. First, we look at his sugar cane."

"Oh, hell, I don't know—"

"With Jean Kirkpatrick."

"Double don't know. I was afraid you were thinking of something like that."

"You want to exercise your voting rights, now?"

The pilot grinned sheepishly as he replied, "You're the skipper. I'll get the plane ready."

"And I," said Bolan, "will get the baggage."

And he would need, he knew, every damned ounce of it.

5

THE SCREW

It was the first sour note in a so-far perfect operation—so it seemed to Project Chief Guido Riappi that he was taking far too much heat for this little foul-up. He said as much to his hard-arm boss, Carlo (the Pip) Papriello, adding almost sadly, "The outfit is getting soft, Pip. I can remember the hard times—I mean the *really* hard times—when you measured your profits by what you had in your hand at the end of the day. Then you sat up all night and watched it. These guys today—I tell you—these guys do a lot of crying over little things."

Riappi was fifty-five. Which did not exactly qualify him as an elder statesman. Papriello, at thirty-seven, was but a single generation behind, yet he'd been hearing these "hard times" stories all his life, forever told as though occurring during some prehistoric era remembered only by the one telling the story. As far as the Pip was concerned, things had always been the same and always would be. But he replied to his boss, "Yeah. I know. That's just the way it goes, Guido. You should try to don't take it pers'nal. So what do they want us to do about it? Hold a wake?"

"They say we should stop everything."

"What?"

"You heard me. Stop everything."

"For how long?"

"Until they, quote, *evaluate*, unquote. I guess that means we get a screw crew."

"Uh huh. So who's going to get screwed?" Papriello asked sullenly.

"Guess," said the boss.

"A couple of tenderfeet got lucky," Papriello growled. "It's no big deal. It don't call for a screw crew. Did you tell 'em that?"

"Sure I told 'em."

"So who're they sending?"

"Didn't say," Riappi replied quietly. He rolled the chair back and crossed his feet atop the desk. "Didn't even say, really, that they were sending anyone. But they didn't have to *say* it, Pip. I could read it. You can read things like that, you know."

The Pip lit a cigar and crossed to the window

where he pulled aside the heavy drapery and gazed stonily at the nothingness that lay outside that window. "It's okay by me, Guido," he growled softly. "To tell the truth, I'm sick of this joint. This whole operation. May as well be in Siberia."

"I ain't heard you complaining about the split," Riappi replied.

"I'm not saying it don't pay well. But, hell, nothing ever changes, does it? The rich just get richer. The poor get older. I don't want to grow old in this joint, Guido. To tell the truth, I been thinking about asking for another slot, somewheres else."

His boss chuckled at that idea. "They might give you one, Pip," he said, with heavy accent on the double meaning. "If I was you, I wouldn't be giving 'em any ideas."

Papriello chuckled also. The implication of Riappi's double meaning was ridiculous. Or was it? He muttered, "It's not that serious, is it, Guido?"

"You never know," the project chief replied, sighing. "You just never know where you stand with these guys, these days. I tell you, Pip, it's not like the old days."

"You know better than that, Guido," Papriello replied softly. "Things never really change."

Riappi sighed again as he said, "Maybe they don't, at that. Maybe they don't. Lookit what the Marinello bunch did to my cousin, Gus. Without cause. Without cause, Pip."

The Pip knew all about cousin Gus Riappi. And there'd been cause, all right. Plenty of cause. But he said to his boss, "I didn't say the outfit hasn't been going to hell for a long time. I just said nothing ever changes, not really. But if they think they're going to send a screw crew down here to rake us over the coals every time a tenderfoot gets lucky—" He stopped talking abruptly and craned his head for a better view of the sky. "Hear that?" he asked Riappi.

"Sounds low," said the boss, getting to his feet and joining Papriello at the window.

It was low, yeah. Circling for a landing. A small, two-engine jet.

"Is that a company plane?" Riappi asked tensely.

"Same kind, looks like," the Pip replied. "A Cessna, I guess."

"That's too damned quick," said Riappi, glancing at his watch. "I just—they couldn't—unless these guys were already on the way when . . ."

"Guess I better get down there and meet them," Papriello decided with a sigh.

"Stop worrying," Riappi said lightly. "This could be anybody. Maybe the farmers. Things are never as bad as they seem."

But the Pip knew better. Things, in this outfit, were always worse than they seemed. And things, the Pip knew, never really changed . . . not for the better.

He left his boss standing at the window and

grabbed a wheelman who was tinkering with a lawnmower in the backyard. "Didn't you see the plane, dummy?" he growled at the guy.

"Yessir, I seen—but I didn't—"

"Better use the limo. These may be very important people. Shit, man, you reek of gasoline—and look at those hands! Never mind, dammit! I'll get 'em, myself!"

He left the guy with his damn greasy hands to play with the lawnmower and personally drove the gleaming Cadillac to the air strip to greet the VIPs. He knew they would be VIPs. They had to be VIPs. Trouble always came in bunches.

The distance was less than five hundred yards through the canefields but still he was a little late in getting there. The pilot was already out of the plane—a vaguely familiar guy—and was helping a leggy knockout of a blonde to the ground.

The babe was wearing abbreviated shorts and not nearly enough halter—and she looked a bit familiar, too.

The Pip was breathing easier, already. This visitation did not bear the marks of a . . .

But then the big guy appeared in the doorway and stepped casually to the ground. A nerve pulsed in Papriello's cheek as he looked at that guy. Tall, cool, very *macho* in trim slacks and Palm Beach blazer, tight shirt open halfway to the waist and a thin silk kerchief knotted against

45

the bare throat. Cold eyes measured everything in sight before finally coming to rest on the Pip— and suddenly all bets were off.

Papriello had never seen this guy before, probably, but he'd seen enough just like him to know where the guy was coming from . . . and what he was coming with . . . and, probably, what he was coming for. The question for the coming was who . . *who,* not what.

The boss of the 'glades hard force got out of the limo and moved quickly forward with hand outstretched.

The pilot took that hand in a warm clasp and casual greeting. "Hi, Pip. How's the swamp fever?"

The son of a bitch knew him.

Pip thought he knew the guy, too. But, shit, you saw so many. . . . "About the same, I guess," the Pip replied, wondering who the hell he was talking to.

The tall guy was pulling baggage off the plane. The blonde was buzzing around making sure he got it all.

Papriello lowered his voice to casually ask the pilot, "Who'd you bring us, this time?"

The guy rolled his eyes as he quietly replied to that indiscreet inquiry. "With those boys, I never ask. The blonde I've seen around Lauderdale. I think she used to be in Miami Vino's stable. You know?"

Sure, the Pip knew all about the late Miami Vino and his fabulous party whores. "Why all

46

the damn baggage?" he asked nervously. "It looks like they've come to stay. Where'd you say you picked them up?"

"Hey, don't put me on the spot, eh?" the pilot muttered. He produced a handkerchief from his hip pocket and mopped his brow with it. "It's an X-rated flight. You know what that means."

Yes, Papriello knew what that meant. It was a flight that never happened. So how could the guy know where he picked somebody up—or where he let them off?

Then the tall guy came over and put the seal on the whole thing.

Without a handshake, without so much as a smile, the guy sealed it all.

"Relax, Pip," that cold voice advised him. "You know why I'm here. Right?"

"Yessir, I guess I do," Papriello solemnly replied.

"You're the head cock around here?"

"Yessir, I am. I report directly to Guido. We've been expecting you. A couple of tender-feet got lucky, that's all. We can handle smart-asses like them. We got a damned hard force here, sir."

"I know you have, Pip." Cold . . . cold as ice. But . . . at the same time, almost friendly. Almost.

"The trouble, sir—"

"It isn't you, Pip. That's all you need to know, for now."

"Yessir. I 'preciate that. I—"

47

The guy was freezing him with those eyes. "It's a lockup. See to it. Nobody comes, nobody goes." He turned those icy eyes to the pilot. "That means you, too, Grimaldi. Get comfortable."

Grimaldi, sure . . . Pip remembered the guy, now. He flew nobody but top brass. So okay. It wasn't Pip at the end of the screw. And that was entirely right, Mr. Hard Ass, that was all the Pip needed to know, for now.

But the chest was nevertheless a bit constricted as he responded to that self-evident authority. "Right, Mr. uh—right, sir, it's locked up until you say different."

"You call me Frankie," said ice-eyes.

"Right, Frankie," said Papriello, feeling much better now—much better, indeed. "And you call me, sir, any damned time you need me."

"You know I will," said the one-man screw crew.

The Pip knew that, sure.

It was simply the way things were. Nothing, Pip also knew, ever really changed.

6

COUP

Bolan was strictly playing the ear. He had not known what sort of reception he would receive in the bold invasion of Santelli's island fortress, nor could he even guess with any certainty as to the mental atmospheres pervading that place in this time and circumstance. Indeed, he could but guess at the circumstances. He did know and understand his enemy, however, and he'd felt that the possibilities for positive results would warrant the risks and uncertainties accompanying the probe.

For probe it was—during those tense early moments. The thing could have gone in any direction. Much depended upon very subtle nuances of the mental climate attending the reception at the airstrip. The whole thing could have been aborted right there—and the timing for such a contingency had been worked down to hairline precision.

But when Grimaldi showed the white handkerchief, Bolan knew that the probe was yielding positive results and that the mission was in "full go" status. The natives were restless, tense, uneasy about the visitation—that was the white handkerchief reading—and that was all the mental atmosphere required by his expert in enemy penetration.

It was not all brass and balls, though, that brought it off. The secret of Mack Bolan's penetration expertise was equally dependent on careful preparation, exhaustive intelligence gathering, and a studied understanding of the enemy. His masquerades, which had already become legendary even in the enemy camps, were no mere matter of costuming and role-playing. They were successful primarily because Bolan knew the enemy better than they knew themselves—and because he knew that their greatest strengths were also their deadliest weaknesses. He operated on those strengths, converted them to his own designs, and strangled the foe with them.

Carlo Papriello was a case in point. The guy had even woven his own noose, placed it over his head, and invited Bolan to pull the lever.

But Carlo the Pip was small game. He would

keep—and he would also become a most willing assistant to the hangman. Twenty years in the outfit but forever a hired gun, the Pip had reached that plateau which awaits every aging gunner, the plateau of diminishing expectations. Gunning was a living, that was all. Fortunes were not made behind the gun. Fortunes were made behind the desk—and Papriello was one of those realists who grudgingly understood his own fate; there was no "desk" in Carlo the Pip's future. He was a realist, yes. And a survivor. And a guy like that was red meat for Mack Bolan's game.

But guys like Papriello were not necessarily stupid, either. Most of them possessed a savage cunning coupled to a hairtrigger mind—and you had to play these guys very carefully.

During the brief drive to the hacienda, the Pip chattily told his important guests, "You came at a good time. Right after the harvest and ahead of the monsoons. Listen, when it rains here . . . well, you have to see it to believe it. They say about fifty inches during the season. That's from . . . oh, about June to maybe October. That plays hell with the Lucifer Ladder, of course. So we have to plan the operations accordingly."

Not so damned "chatty," at that.

The guy was testing the visitor, probing his depth of familiarity with the local game. He had not mentioned the Lucifer Ladder all that casually. Bolan had heard whispered echoes of that strange expression. Indeed, they had brought

51

him here. But he could only faintly guess at the meaning.

And this was no time for faint guesses.

Bolan let it pass without a bite, coldly replying, "Exactly why I'm here, Pip."

"Sure, I understand," was the quiet response. And there was no further conversation until they reached the house.

It was a large island, connected to another land mass a quarter mile to the east by a narrow land bridge, almost entirely under agriculture except for a small airstrip and the residence compound clustered at the south shore. The latter consisted of a two-story Spanish-style stucco with a red-tile roof, several small bungalows, some outbuildings, and a four-stall garage with overhead living quarters—all enclosed within wire fencing except at the waterfront.

Papriello explained, "The farm settlement is on the north side. Only two permanent families, the Eddingtons and the Winklers. Eddington is the manager but we got nothing to do with him. He takes his orders straight from Mr. Santelli's front office. And, of course, they're not wise."

"Lot of cane, here," Bolan quietly commented.

"Yessir, I guess they use itinerant labor to work the fields. Come and go, you know. Blacks, mostly, I guess. Got a bunch of shacks on the north side, they use while they're here. Anyway, we never see any of that unless we need to." He raised his eyebrows as he added, "You know what I mean."

Bolan did not know, no, but interesting possibilities were being presented. He said, "It's a good cover, yeah."

"Profitable, too," the Pip informed him. "I mean, legit profit. Sugar prices have gone out of sight on the commodity markets."

Bolan smiled faintly as he commented, "You watch things like that, eh?"

The guy colored slightly and growled, "Not really, no. We got enough to worry about, as it is. But it's not all joy, you know. A guy sometimes thinks of the future. To tell the truth, I been thinking about buying up a piece of that market."

"You could lose your ass playing another man's game," Bolan said quietly.

"It beats going stir crazy," Pip insisted. "To tell the truth, sir, I'm not really happy here."

Bolan had already deduced that much. He told the guy, "Cheer up, Pip. Things are changing."

He knew that he had struck a nerve somewhere with that comment. Papriello did not respond vocally but the eyes told it all. The guy was a realist, yeah . . . and a survivor.

So was Bolan.

And the reality of the moment was that he had entered an armed camp which was fairly bristling with enemy guns. The bungalows and the garage apartment were serving as barracks and obviously they could house a formidable force. Bolan counted a dozen armed men in the first casual sweep of the eyes, scattered between the hacienda and the shoreline. Perhaps another dozen would be found to the rear. God only knew how many more were lurking about under cover within the many buildings.

It was not a situation to encourage reckless tactics. One false step, a single improper nuance, could bring immediate disaster.

How these guys would love a whack at Mack Bolan's head. Presumably all the bounties were still intact, despite the fact that most of those who'd posted the bounties were no longer among the living. More than the money, though, much more to guys like these, would be the fame and prestige to descend upon those responsible for placing Bolan's head in a paper sack.

This particular bunch looked bored as hell, at the moment—and this circumstance would be Bolan's best key. Obviously the entire force was being kept under close wraps within the island hard site. Evidence of faint-hearted attempts to provide recreational facilities could be seen here and there: a rough lawn-bowling course, couple of sagging and bedraggled badminton nets, an abandoned volley ball, lawn darts, a brace of canoes at the shoreline—any or all of which would prove faint recreation, indeed, for the likes of these street soldiers.

The way those guys were checking out Jean Kirkpatrick told another obvious story: they were not accustomed to seeing females around here.

Bolan growled to his guide, "How long, Pip?"

"How long what, sir?"

"No women."

"Oh hell. What's a woman, sir?"

"That's going to change, too," the VIP visitor promised the head cock.

That struck another nerve, as Bolan knew it would. The word would be all over that hard site before Bolan could get inside the house.

The new boss of Santelli Island was going to be a very popular leader . . . even before his installation.

Guido Riappi came to the front porch to greet the arrivals. Bolan's mental file had the guy made instantly. Riappi's cousin Gus had once been heir to the criminal empire of Maryland boss Arnie (the Farmer) Castiglione but Gus died in disgrace, instead, after allowing Bolan to reach right under his nose to execute Sir Edward Stuart, chairman of the mob's Caribbean Carousel.

Things had not gone too well for Guido after that, either. It seems that he complained too bitterly and to the wrong people about his cousin's treatment at the hands of the mob's ruling council in New York. To Bolan's knowledge, the present assignment was Guido's first "important" berth since the fall of cousin Gus. One thing certainly had emerged from that experience: Guido

Riappi had learned the meaning of uncertainty and insecurity in a cannibal society.

The guy looked none the worse for any of it. Fat, pink, almost a jolly figure in white duck trousers and flowered sportshirt. Not so jolly, though, beneath that flabby exterior. Guido Riappi had made his reputation at the expense of certain longshoremen groups along the eastern seaboard, first as a union organizer and legbreaker, later as a feared enforcer of mob authority under Castiglione in the Baltimore area. Federal authorities were certain, but could not prove, that the savage Wolf of Baltimore was directly responsible for some fifty murders and scores of lesser brutalities during a single period of unrest in the late sixties.

You'd never think it, to look at the guy.

He came at Bolan all smiles and good will, obviously getting the size of his visitor in a single glance and moving quickly to establish hospitable relations.

Bolan introduced the lady but not himself, saving that formality for a more intimate moment. He turned the lady over to a grateful Pip for a guided tour then wrapped an arm about Riappi and gently but firmly led him inside while busying that worried mind with quiet pleasantries and persuasive reassurances.

"Relax, Guido, relax. I know how it must look. But things are never as bad as they seem. Right? You've got your boys too tight, though. They're going to shatter. First thing I want you to do is loosen up a bit around here."

"I been thinking about that, yeah. Trouble is, how to do it? I can't be bringing busloads of broads out here on one-night stands. You know how they talk. Sure as hell I can't turn the joint into a live-in whorehouse. Same time, I can't take a chance on letting these boys run around town and all the damn trouble they can get theirselves into. First you know, I got a fed behind every bush and movie cameras and the whole bit. Course, I know, I can't keep these boys penned up forever, neither. They lose their edge, don't they. I guess that's why the fuckup this morning. I hope you got some ideas about that."

The guy, yeah, had learned his lessons in uncertainty and insecurity. He was taking first crack, inviting the hotshot from the headshed to flex some muscle in a hospitable atmosphere.

Guido was giving room.

Mack Bolan was willing to take it.

The conversation had taken them through a heavily draped and gloomy lounge area and into Guido's office, equally depressing. The whole place smelled mustily of mildew and tropical rot.

Bolan twitched his nose and asked, "How do you stand this?"

"This what?" the guy replied, genuinely baffled.

"This joint is like a pharaoh's tomb. Can't

you get some fresh air and sunlight in here?"

"Oh, say, it's six of one and half a dozen of another. We got no air conditioning here. Open the joint up and you got bugs and sweltering heat. Couple of days on this rock, believe me, and this house will start feeling real comfortable to you. I hardly ever go outside anymore."

"Maybe that's the trouble," Bolan replied coldly, giving the guy a flat, hard eye for the first time.

The hit scored. Riappi dropped his gaze and turned his back to the visitor, sinking quietly into a chair at the desk. Bolan had taken more room than the guy had offered. But the attitude told plainly that he was prepared to give that, also.

"Maybe you're right," Riappi muttered. "So what do you want me to do?"

The Executioner had landed.

And the situation—for the moment, at least—was well in hand. Santelli Island had itself a new boss.

7

THE TURF

"I have the information on that real estate," April Rose reported to Brognola. "The purchaser was Atlantica Holding Company. Santelli's name does not appear on the deed but he is an officer in every company under the Atlantica umbrella. And this one, particularly, Resorts Atlantica, is a subsidiary of Atlantica Holding and Santelli is chairman of the board. Resorts Atlantica picked up the smaller piece called Satan's Hammock at the same time and at a fantastic price. Actually, price seems to have been no object for either sale. They paid more than double the market value for both pieces."

"I wonder why," Brognola mused.

"Has my nose out of joint, too," April said. "It took a bit of political footwork, I suspect, to engineer the Satan's Hammock buy. The site had been under the protection of a state commission for the past twenty years. The preserve status was canceled just a few weeks before the deal was closed."

"What were they preserving?"

"It had been the site of an archeological dig. But apparently everything of value had been removed years ago. According to the petition for abandonment, the site had not been worked during the past seven years."

Brognola sniffed and murmured, "Indian mounds?"

April shook her head, explaining, "Paleolithic studies. That's Stone Age stuff. They'd been investigating something called a cenote. What's a cenote?"

"Beat's me," the chief growled. "Why don't you look it up?"

"I tried. My dictionary doesn't know a thing about it."

"Then I suggest you consult an archeologist."

"The call is already in," she replied, smiling.

"My, you're feeling peachy," the chief fed observed wryly. "What became of that Pitiful Pearl I had around here all morning?"

"I don't know," April admitted cheerily. "I just sense that—well I have the feeling that it's starting to break open."

Brognola grinned. "Couldn't have a thing to

do with the fact that we got the wires back on our man," he said.

" 'Course not," April said, smiling back at him. "I'm a professional. I don't get emotionally involved in my work."

The chief was about to say something cute in reply to that outrageous lie when the technician at the communications desk brought in a new one. "Flash from Flypaper," he announced. "They're airborne again. And you won't believe this!"

"What?" Brognola inquired, rising quickly to his feet.

"Says he has a Mr. Smith aboard. That translates to Guido Riappi. They're enroute to Miami International. ETA is eleven o'clock. He wants an official reception for Mr. Smith."

"Tell him we're covering it!" Brognola snapped, turning then to April with a baffled frown. "How the hell . . . ?"

"Our man is *operating*!" she exulted.

"Yeah, but, how the hell . . .?" Brognola stalked to the communications console and commanded the technician, "Cut me in!" He donned a headset and spoke into the mouthpiece: "Flypaper, this is Alice. What the hell is going down?"

He stared thoughtfully at April while the report rattled his earphone, then: "Okay, I guess. Good work. Pass that along. How can we support?"

Another thoughtful stare at April, then: "I

guess I can live with that. I just hope you guys can."

"He's operating, all right," Brognola told April. "Striker is still on the island. He's taken the whole joint over. Riappi thinks he's on his way to a meeting in Miami."

She bit her lip as she prompted, "And . . . ?"

"And that's all I know. How the hell am I supposed to know what that guy is doing?"

"I've seen him operate at close range," April murmured.

"So've I," the chief said heavily. "And that's what scares the hell out of me."

"What was it you said you could live with?"

"Inactivity," Brognola fumed. "He's demanding plenty of room, in which his miracles are to be performed."

"Then we'll just have to give him the room," April decided, very uncharacteristically. She caught the disbelieving glint in the chief's eyes. "No, I mean it. I'm very grown up about all this, now. But that isn't what is really bothering you. What is?"

Brognola's eyes fled to the ceiling of the mobile command center as he told her, "Flypaper says there's at least fifty guns on that island. He sounded, uh, very concerned."

April said, in a very small voice, "I see."

"Striker wants us to pull back and confine our activities to electronic surveillance. Absolutely no physical intrusion."

"Until when?"

Her telephone rang. Brognola seemed to welcome the interruption. April glowered at the phone for a moment then picked it up and announced, "Justice Three-Ten."

A cultured voice in there told her, "This is Louis Cardinez."

Brognola had turned away and was going into a huddle with a couple of his marshals. He was obviously deeply concerned about the recent turn of this mission.

April was concerned, too, but she was learning how to handle it. Professional involvement . . . that was the key.

She composed her voice and told the caller, "Oh, yes, thank you, Doctor, for returning my call."

"I understand there is a matter of some urgency. To whom am I speaking, please?"

April identified herself, then asked, "What is a cenote?"

The good doctor seemed to think that someone may be having a joke at his expense . . . and he was going along with the gag. "I believe that's a vulgarism for a hundred dollar bill, isn't it?"

April giggled indulgently, reaffirmed her identity, and told the man, "We are in the midst of an investigation, a highly important investigation, and we have come across a reference to a cenote." She spelled it. "I can't find the word in the dictionary. But I understand it to be an archeological term. The university information center referred me to you as the resident authority on archeological matters."

"I see. Yes, well, you don't find the word in your dictionary perhaps because it is not properly a part of the English language. Nor is it an archeological term, *per se*. You need to speak to a geologist."

She said, "I need only very general information. Can't you help me?"

He was sounding mildly exasperated. "What do you wish to know?"

"What is a cenote?"

Doctor Cardinez sighed as he replied, "The word comes to us from the Maya. To put it succinctly, a cenote is merely a fresh water well or reservoir."

"Let's put it another way," April persisted. "As an archeologist, why would you be interested in such a thing?"

"First let's define the term more precisely," Cardinez said, apparently getting into the scholarly spirit. "Cenotes are quite common along the Yucatan Peninsula and some have been discovered here in Florida, most notably in the southwestern region. They are peculiar to geological formations featuring thick limestone strata. A cenote occurs when a surface of limestone becomes undermined and collapses, revealing underground water which has collected in natural reservoirs beneath the porous surface. I presume that your interest is confined to our local phenomena?"

"That's right, yes. And why archeology?"

"Well, you see, for many primitive peoples, the cenotes represented their only source of fresh water, especially during long dry periods. You can understand, then, why the primitives would attach holy significance to such phenomena. Water, my dear, is the source of all life. And it has not always been in plentiful supply for those who depend upon it for survival. You can imagine the impression made upon a primitive mind when a thirsty and dying tribesman finds the earth collapsing beneath his feet to reveal a seemingly infinite supply of potable water."

"Yes, well—"

"The primitives attached great supernatural significance to such phenomena. Some cenotes have been found to extend to considerable depths, often fed by underground streams. It was a widespread custom during ancient times to drop all manner of precious objects into them as an offering to the gods. The custom survives today, though few of us really understand why we feel so compelled to drop coins into wishing wells, manmade fountains, and the like. The ancients even gave human sacrifices to their cenotes. So you can understand the archeological significance. A very old cenote can become a rich source of human artifacts dating back to Paleolithic times and even beyond."

"That's very interesting," April murmured. "Do you have personal knowledge of any such Paleolithic studies being conducted here in Florida?"

"I believe that you have something specific in mind," Cardinez replied, becoming just a shade defensive.

"I have Satan's Hammock in mind," she said bluntly.

He coughed delicately and said, "Yes, well, that one was quite a disappointment. The cenote discovered on Satan's Hammock is relatively modern. The age has been calculated at something less than four hundred years so there is no possible Paleolithic significance. A few scattered artifacts left by Calusa peoples who may have camped at the site from time to time were found but, you see, surface water has been abundant on the Florida peninsula for the past five thousand years. Cenotes are significant to local inhabitants only during periods when fresh surface water is in relatively short supply, during dry climactic periods. There were many such periods during Paleolithic times, of prolonged duration, so naturally any existing cenotes would have strongly influenced the distribution of human populations. What I am saying, in brief, is that Paleolithic peoples tended to cluster and settle around sources of fresh water."

"And Florida had Paleolithic peoples—Stone-Agers?"

"Oh yes. The archeological finds at Little Salt Spring, for example, have convincingly dated human presence in the area at roughly fifteen thousand years."

"That's in Florida?"

"Oh yes. Near Charlotte Harbor, on the gulf side."

"Is Little Salt Spring a cenote? I thought you said they were fresh water."

"Little Salt Spring deteriorated during the mineralization process, during relatively modern times—an almost inevitable process. Satan's Hammock presents a rather striking contrast, due perhaps to its relative youth. You would have to ask a geologist about that. In most other respects, the two cenotes are strikingly similar. In each case, the original reservoir has become obscured by the formation of a larger surface basin which has filled with water from the cenote, presenting the appearance of an ordinary pond or small lake. But this is quite common, of course, particularly in areas such as—"

"I don't understand that, Doctor."

"What? Oh. Well, viewed from the surface, the observer sees only a small body of water, in no way distinguishable from any small spring-fed lake or pond, with which this state abounds. It's an old saying in these parts that you can stamp on the ground most anywhere and strike a spring."

"I see."

"Yes. Not even a trained observer—a geologist, for example—would suspect the presence of a cenote occurring somewhere on the floor of that basin. Not until he donned diving apparatus and thoroughly explored the bottom of the lake or pond or whatever."

"Then how would he recognize—exactly what would he find down there to tell him that this is a cenote?"

"That would vary, depending upon the size and constitution of the subterranean chamber. In the case of Little Salt Spring—Satan's Hammock, as well—it is a dramatic and stirring discovery. He would find a vertical underwater cavern, quite deep—eight to ten times deeper, in fact, than the lake above it, with an entrance measuring some twenty meters wide."

"That's uh . . ."

"Roughly sixty feet in diameter. May I inquire as to the Justice Department's interest in Satan's Hammock?"

April countered with a question of her own. "Are you aware that it has been abandoned as an archeological preserve?"

"Oh yes. There's nothing irregular about that, let me assure you. The academic community abandoned the project years ago."

"Are you also aware that the site has recently been purchased by a resorts corporation at an unbelievably high price?"

The archeologist replied thoughtfully, "No, I

was not aware of that. As to the price, it would be difficult to assign a dollar value to such a phenomenon, especially if one is thinking in terms of a tourist attraction."

"It would be an attraction, then?"

"Oh, good lord, yes! Have you ever been to Silver Springs?"

"I'm afraid not."

"Fabulously popular place. A goldmine. The early Tarzan movies were filmed there. Satan's Hammock could be beautifully developed along similar lines. Of course, there could be an access problem, when one is thinking of hordes of visitors. Presently the hammock is accessible only via water. But the large island just to the north of the hammock has automobile access. And I suppose another land bridge could be built to connect the two. But it would take an enormous investment, wouldn't it?"

"I suppose so," April agreed. "Well . . . you have been a delight. Thanks for the cooperation, Doctor Cardinez. Oh . . . one more thing . . . have you actually been there?"

"Satan's Hammock? Oh yes, certainly, many times. But not for quite a long time. Why do you ask?"

"Just how deep is that cenote?"

"The main chamber extends to a depth of some sixty meters below its opening."

"I'm not, uh, too quick at metric conversions, Doctor."

"Well a meter is roughly one yard. You can

figure it that way, if you're not going for a precision measurement."

"So it's almost two hundred feet deep."

"In the main chamber, yes."

"Wait a minute, now. Are you suggesting that there is more than one cavern down there?"

"Satan's Hammock sits atop a network of subterranean chambers, my dear. A number of underground streams converge at the main chamber. How do you think it came to be called *Satan's Hammock?* There may be no end to the thing. But there is no practical method to explore beyond the main chamber . . . not for very far . . . unless one is equipped with unlimited funds and boundless curiosity as well as great courage. However, as I mentioned earlier, it has been positively established that there is no archeological significance to the phenomenon."

April thanked the good doctor again and broke the connection.

Brognola was staring at her from his desk, having obviously long ago concluded the conference with his gunslingers.

She'd lost track of the time, and the conversation with Cardinez had covered considerably more ground than had been anticipated. *Ask a simple question, April . . .*

She turned a thoughtfully puckered face to her boss and said, "Well I'll be darned."

"What did you get?" he asked her.

"I'm not sure," she replied. "But I think . . ."

well, maybe . . . it's just possible that what I got is . . ."

"What?" he prompted.

"Lucifer's Ladder," she said quietly.

8

THE TAKEOVER

Bolan's psy-war tactics had made a quivering mess of Guido Riappi. The guy's recent history had apparently made him especially vulnerable to artfully applied pressure—and Bolan was a master of the art.

When he "revealed" the true nature of his visit, the one-time legbreaker came apart at the seams.

"I don't personally like this, Guido."

"What don't you like, Frankie?"

"I was never one to stand and smirk over another man's broken body. Especially a man who has been a brother for so long."

"I don't think I get you. Do I get you?"

"I guess you get me, Guido."

That was when the seams ripped. They were all inside seams, of course, but wholly visible through the eyes. The guy gulped air as though he were trying to feed a fire down below and he came halfway out of the chair twice before finally settling in a defeated heap. Then nothing moved but the lips, like waxen flaps reciting some long-feared litany. "Just like Gus. Just like Gus, dammit, Frankie . . . why do they do this? It's crazy! Why do they do this?"

Bolan gently explained, "You reach a certain level, Guido, and there's no other way out. You know that. In this outfit, you move either head first or feet first. If someone figures the head isn't working right then there's only one way they can move you."

"It's working, dammit, the head's working. It's been going like a dream. One small fuckup, that's all, just one. And it ain't even hours old before they've decided something's wrong with the head. Who're *they* to decide? Huh? Who th' hell are *they*?"

"They're the men with the investment, Guido. Hey—there's nothing personal. You know that."

"Sure I know that, Frankie. Hey—have I said a word in anger to you—personally to you?"

Of course he hadn't. That would come later, if at all, in a final fling for survival. At the moment, Riappi was deeply grateful to have a show of sympathy from his executioner. That was something to work with. And Bolan allowed him that much.

"We're men, Guido. Brothers. We don't need anger."

"Right. You're right. Listen, if I could just *talk* to someone—if I could just *show* them how wrong they are—listen, I could turn this thing around."

"I told 'em that, Guido. I told 'em, the man has been a brother, a good brother, for a long time. Forget the thing with Gus. It was his only trespass. And, after all, there was blood between them. But you know, Guido, you've been like on probation here. I mean, some things are hard to forget. And it don't take much to bring back unpleasant memories. I give it to you flat and straight. They think you're dead on your ass. They think you've gotten fat and soft, especially in the head. That's why I was sent."

"I can't believe this, Frankie. I really can't believe this. I'm not soft in the head. You can see that. Why can't they?"

"There's all this heavy investment, Guido. You know how they get when big bucks are on the line. Hey—don't we know how they get?"

"Sure, sure. The bucks are all that count, isn't that right? See, I feel the same way. I want the same things they want. Listen, I still think I could talk—who should I call—who's the best—?"

"No calls, Guido. Hey. It would make me look bad." Bolan made an exaggerated study of his watch. "How long have I been here? About ten minutes? That's not very damn long, is it? Hell, maybe I'm not even here yet."

There was no mistaking that offer, not to a wiseguy. Bolan thought for a moment the guy was going to drop to his knees and kiss his hand. He did it symbolically, anyway, raising his own chubby hand to his lips and speaking past it as he gasped, "God you are a hell of a *man*, Frankie. You are a *man*! But what should I do?"

"If it was me, Guido," Bolan replied quietly, "and I'd heard a rumor that someone was being sent for me, I don't think I'd make any phone calls. I think I'd want to talk to the senders, myself, face to face, man to man, before they knew I knew. And if I had a plane sitting out here on the airstrip, and a pilot just waiting for some flight orders . . . well, hey, that's what I'd do, Guido. I'd go talk to those men."

"Are they in Miami Beach? Is that where? At Muscatel's?"

"That's where I'd go," Bolan said softly. "And I'd do it before a certain somebody got here. What time you got, Guido? I guess my watch is fast. I shouldn't be arriving here for another half-hour or so."

The guy was ready to lick his feet. "I won't forget this, Frankie. I swear, I—"

"It never happened!" Bolan said harshly. "Don't you never forget that! I never saw you, you never saw me, you never heard my name! You got that? One last thing . . . you go any-

75

where but Miami Beach and you'll have my shadow on your ass 'til the day you die."

"God, I wouldn't do that to you, Frankie. Anyway, I know I can straighten this out."

Ten minutes later the guy was off the island and "Frankie" was in command.

Every man there knew precisely what had happened. And there was nothing but admiring glances and respectful attention for the new project boss.

"Now I want to see this golden goose of ours," he told Papriello.

"I can hardly wait to show you, sir. Do you know that Guido has never seen it? He never saw it, sir."

But Mack Bolan would.

Yes, indeed.

Mack Bolan was going to get the ten-billion-dollar tour.

9

THE RIDE

The "house boss" was one Johnny Paoli, a more or less trustworthy middle-aged thug who had a reputation for doing precisely what he was told to do, nothing more and nothing less. The guy was obviously a bit deficient upstairs but he could understand an order and he possessed the brawn if not the brains to make an order stick.

Bolan took him aside and patiently explained the new pecking order at Santelli Island. Then he told him, "You watch after the lady, Johnny. Nobody touches her. Nobody comes in the damn house, period, while I'm out of it."

"I got that," Paoli grunted.

"You keep it."

"I got it and I'll keep it, right."

"No phone calls."

"No phone calls, right."

"Any calls coming in for Guido, you just say he's not here. He's not here. That's all."

"Guido's not here right now."

"That's it exactly. You never heard of Frankie Cavaretta."

"Right, I never heard of that guy. Who the hell is Frankie Cavaretta, boss?"

"That's me, Johnny. But you never heard of me."

"Oh, right, I never heard of you. I get that. I'll keep that, too."

"I'm going to be depending on you, Johnny, to keep my house clean."

"Depend on me, right." The guy was counting it off with the fingers. "Take care of the lady. Nobody comes in. No phone calls. Guido's not here right now. I never heard of that Cavaretta guy."

Bolan patted that disturbed head then he took the lady aside and told her, "You cool it. I mean, take a bath, anything but—"

"I didn't come out here to cool anything," she protested.

"We play my game, first," he insisted. "Once that one is tight enough, we'll take a look at yours. You have my word on that. For now, cool it."

She batted those huge eyes as she replied, "Okay. Your word is good enough for me. But don't be long, huh? Maybe I have a tight schedule, too."

"You want to talk about it right now?" he asked quietly.

"Not right now." She kissed him hard on the mouth then ran up the stairs.

Bolan watched her into the house then he signaled Papriello with the eyes and went off for a tour of the territory. The head gunner led him to a small outbuilding at the center of the compound, explaining, "This is what we call the portal. Guido never came any farther than this. I think he has a head problem. You know, one of them, whattayacallit, phobia."

A big, mean-looking guy responded to a rap at the door. "This is your new boss," Papriello told the guy. "Say hello to Frankie Cavaretta."

The keeper of the portal flashed a huge grin at the new boss-in-residence and showed how quick the word can travel in a closed system. "Hi, boss. Bring on them crazy ladies. I'm ready any time."

Bolan showed how a photographic memory operates by quickly scrolling through the mental mugfile and withdrawing a handle for the guy. "Hi, Rocky," he replied breezily. "Tonight's the night, so save your energy."

The guy was one Lucian "the Rock" Vesperanza, another alumnus of the old Castiglione family—never anything more than a street soldier, a button man, but among the most dependably mean of the lot. And Bolan was beginning to understand what had become of the old Castiglione power nucleus. It seemed that they were alive and well in Florida. For the moment, anyway.

Vesperanza was showing a wall-to-wall smile, ignoring Papriello's obvious discomfort over his unpardonable familiarity with the new boss.

The Pip threw an apologetic glance at Bolan as he explained, "The boys are just glad you're here, Frankie."

"Sure, I know," Bolan replied easily.

"We're going across," Pip told Vesperanza.

The grinning thug stepped back into the interior of the building and the other two moved inside. Nothing was in there but an overstuffed chair, a folding cot, an orange crate doing service as a table, and a transistor radio. There were no windows. Walls and ceiling were unfinished, rough. The flooring was unpainted plywood. A filthy throw rug concealed one 4 x 6 square of that flooring which in turn concealed a steep subterranean stairway, narrow and dimly lit.

Papriello flashed a quick smile at Bolan and led the way down.

The angle of descent seemed to be just about due south from the hole in the floor. Bolan counted twenty-nine iron steps, calculating the penetration southward at maybe fifteen feet before he came onto a broad landing, a ninety-degree turn to due west, and another twenty-nine-step descent.

And though he had suspected some such arrangement, Bolan was mentally unprepared for that which lay at the bottom of that descent.

It was a large, dome-shaped cavern—roughly circular and measuring perhaps thirty feet across—sloping walls converging to form the domed roof which stood some fifty feet above a subterranean pool occupying the bottom, wall to wall. The stairway from the surface ended at a steel catwalk anchored into the stone walls at about ten feet above the water level and leading to another tunnel-like cavern at the south wall, from which was trickling a thin waterfall into the pool.

Papriello spoke his first words since entering the stairwell. "Ain't it enough to blow your mind?" he asked almost reverently.

Bolan quietly agreed with that comment, then asked: "How deep is the water?"

"I never went down to find out," the Pip replied, chuckling. "But they tell me there might not be no bottom."

"Everything has a bottom," Bolan growled.

"They tell me," Papriello replied in a confidential tone, "that the water gets warmer the farther down you go. Maybe it bottoms in hell."

Bolan said, very soberly, "Maybe it does."

"To tell the truth, it gives me the spooks,

sometimes. I'm not superstitious, you know. But a place like this makes you wonder, sometimes."

Bolan understood the feeling. From such natural wonders, perhaps, were born all the primitive religions. He said, gruffly, "Let's go, Pip."

The guy grinned sheepishly and led the way around the catwalk to the horizontal cavern. He fumbled along the wall until he found a lightswitch and warned, "Watch your head here, Boss," and stepped through the entrance.

Water was running ankle deep along the stone floor. Bolan had to bend almost double to move through the shallow tunnel before emerging into another rock-walled vault, some six to ten feet farther along. But this vault was obviously man-made, and very recently so—or, more properly, man-enlarged. Walls and ceiling had been pushed back and reinforced with steel bars supporting steelmesh sheeting. A low platform led to another horizontal cavern—or probably it was a continuation of the original—in which had been constructed a small monorail system.

"From this point," Papriello said, grinning, "we travel in style."

The open, bullet-shaped car would seat six in a single-file configuration. The Pip took the driver's seat and Bolan dropped in behind him.

"We call this the tunnel of love," Papriello said lightly. He chuckled, adding, "But I ain't had no lovin' down here, yet."

The whole feeling was that of a "ride" in an

amusement park. But Bolan was not feeling particularly amused by the experience.

"Just keep your arms inside," Papriello warned as he set the car in motion. "Especially on the curves. There's a couple of narrow squeaks along here."

The car was obviously electrically powered. The ride was smooth and quiet, if a bit slow. The air was good and the temperature comfortable. A guy could close the eyes and have no sensation of moving along a tunnel at some thirty feet or more below the surface of the earth.

But Bolan was not closing the eyes and he was feeling anything but comfort. He was moving, he knew, into something fantastic and satanically threatening—with no superstitious nonsense involved. Not that Mack Bolan did not believe in the powers of good and evil. Satan, he knew, was alive and well—embodied in certain mortals. The *true* Lucifer's Ladder would be found in that mental passageway linking flesh and blood human beings to the pits of hell—and it drew all its power, he also knew, from the good intentions of the meek.

He knew, also, that the meek would never inherit *this* earth—not while that linkage was there.

Bolan had, indeed, submerged his very life into that proposition.

And he had been busily severing links wherever he could find them.

He had, however, never expected to find them in such a place as this. And, being mortal himself—he had to wonder if he had finally found the link which would sever Mack Bolan, instead.

10

ISLAND X

This joint was staggering to the imagination. The chamber must have measured some fifty feet long by a hundred and fifty feet wide, with a depth that defied casual estimates . . . maybe equal to an eight- to ten-story building.

And that was about what these crazy people were engineering down here in this hole in the ground: a framework building, fashioned of steel and anchored directly into the rock sides at each level, with steel ladders and catwalks going off at various angles to hook the levels together. Great massive doors suggesting airlocks or some type of watertight system were emplaced right into the rock facings at various levels. An overhead crane on rails, set high into the arched dome, was presently lowering a section of prefabricated steelmesh into the depths. Somewhere down there an air compressor was operating and Bolan could hear the sucking rumble of great volumes of water in motion—in fact, that was all that could be heard. The whole thing was brightly lit and apparently under good atmospheric controls but the noise level in that hole was almost unbearable.

The monorail from Santelli Island had brought them in at the top level, about ten feet below the crane rails. Two men dressed in limp khaki and wearing yellow hardhats stood in a glass cubicle at the far side, fussing with a large roll of blueprints.

Papriello had to tug at Bolan's sleeve to get his attention. He mouthed the words, "Over here," and led the way to the cubicle.

It was a control room with exotic electronic panels and even a computer terminal . . . and it was soundproofed, thank God. The hardhats barely acknowledged their presence, giving a flick of grudging welcome with the eyes then returning to an agitated study of the blueprints.

"What the hell is going on here?" Papriello demanded. "Where is everybody? What's all the damned noise?"

Those guys were not "boys." They were bonafide engineers and obviously knew what they were about. One of them announced, without looking up, "Blowout at a hundred and twenty feet. We've contained it. Now we're trying to determine the extent."

"Can you fix it?" Papriello wanted to know.

"Sure, we can fix it."

"How much damned delay are we talking about?"

"You'll have to talk to the chief about that," the guy said. He raised a level stare to Bolan. "Beat it, eh. This is a serious problem. We have no time for tourists."

"Watch your smart mouth!" Papriello yelled, eyes blazing with outrage.

"It's okay," Bolan said easily. "You heard the man. He's busy. Let's go."

They returned to the catwalk and went through one of the strange, airlock-type doors into a short passageway which shortly became a staircase almost identical to the one at the other portal. The noise was once again behind them. Papriello puffed, "Sorry 'bout that damned smart mouth, Frankie. When this job is finished, I'm tellin' you the truth, I'm going to have my innings with those people."

Bolan dismissed the incident with a breezy, "So long as they give us what we want, Pip."

"Yeah, well, I'm going to give 'em what *they* want as soon as it's done."

The guy was still panting with suppressed rage when they reached the surface. This portal was simply a small cement-block housing built around the top of the stairs. They exited into bright sunshine and a charmingly tropical scene.

The lagoon which Grimaldi had spotted from the air lay some fifty yards to the south of the portal, a beautiful crescent-shaped inlet lined with palm trees and other luxuriant vegetation. Also lining that verdant shoreline and snuggling beneath the palms were a dozen or more small hut-like structures reminiscent of a South Seas island village. At the very center of the crescent stood a long rectangular building with a low roofline, behind which rose a high tower bristling with radio antennae and supporting a covered platform. It was a watch tower, pure and simple, the kind you would see at prison walls. Two guys were up there with shotguns. It was also equipped, Bolan noted, with searchlights.

"Nice, really nice," Bolan-Cavaretta murmured as he stopped to light a cigarette.

His guide told him, "You should've seen it before they cut the banks away. This was a spring lake, you know. I mean, not connected to the 'glades. They had to screw it up. Water control, you know."

No, Bolan did not know and could not risk asking the obvious question. But he could see, now, the very obvious restructuring which had converted a spring lake into an everglades lagoon. The body of water had been considerably enlarged beyond its original western bank by the simple expedient of lowering the land elevation at that end and allowing the two bodies of water to meet.

"Water control," he echoed quietly.

"It's been drivin' 'em nuts," Papriello elaborated. "There's about a dozen underground streams down there. They get one plugged up and another busts loose. I guess that's the problem right now. Guy said a blowout."

Bolan would have loved to ask why so much time and obvious expense was going into that hole. Surely it was not all for the sake of an underground link to Santelli Island. And he was thinking of those huge watertight doors dotting that fabulous hole in the ground. He said, "They're pumping it out through the lagoon, eh?"

"Well, they call it diverting. They can run it four or five different ways. The lagoon, I guess, is the failsafe. I've seen currents running out of there . . . must be twenty, thirty miles an hour. I mean, real gushers. There's a lot of water down there."

"Where the hell's it coming from?" Bolan muttered, sounding only vaguely interested.

The guy shrugged his shoulders as he replied to that. "I never asked. I just know it's worse during the rainy season."

A stout man of perhaps fifty-five emerged from one of the shoreline huts and trudged toward them. He wore a loose-fitting jumpsuit and a hardhat. Papriello had spotted the approach, too, and said, "Speak of the devil. Here's the guy to ask about that. He's the chief engineer. Takes his orders straight from the top, you know what I mean, so we don't usually have much to say to each other. He's a doctor of something, engineering I guess. Name's Anderson, everybody calls him Doc."

"Yeah, I know," Bolan lied. He wished to hell he did know something. And he was reading nothing but trouble from a parallel chain of command.

Papriello called ahead to the guy when he was about twenty paces off, "Hey, Doc, it's terrible, eh. Not another damn blowout, eh."

Anderson ignored the comment, possessing eyes only for the tall stranger. "Not another damned tourist," he said tiredly, speaking perhaps only to himself.

Papriello stiffened defensively and growled back, "Listen, Doc, this is—"

But Bolan cut into that before the introduction could be made. "Guess it's a bad time for sightseeing," he acknowledged lightly. "Don't let me get in your way, Anderson. I can make it another time."

The guy gave him a go-to-hell look then turned the cold gaze upon Papriello. "You've got to do something about your God-damned turnkeys, Pip. I lost two more workers this morning with busted heads. And it had nothing to do with the blowout. You put a rein on those gorillas. I mean that."

A turnkey, Bolan immediately noted, was the term used for a jailer or prison guard. And that damned watchtower . . .

"I'll look into it," Papriello promised the chief

engineer, with a defensive glance at Bolan. "I was going to ask . . . there's nobody in the hole. Where are they?"

"They're in the hall. It's looking like they'll get another day of rest, so dammit let them rest. An exhausted workman isn't worth his rations. And speaking of rations . . ."

"Yeah, yeah," Papriello said quickly, "we're making a lot of changes." Another glance at Bolan. "I can promise you that."

The chief engineer stalked off without another glance at Bolan, obviously heading toward the portal.

"His time is coming, too, maybe," Papriello raged under his breath.

"All things in their time, Pip," Bolan said coolly.

"I noticed you didn't want to be introduced. I hope that means what I think it means."

"Like I said, all things in their time," Bolan replied, but saying only with the eyes what the guy really wanted to hear.

Papriello gnashed his teeth as he said, "I can hardly wait. Listen, these guys treat us like we're shit on their shoes."

"Didn't I tell you there would be some changes around here?"

"To tell the truth, sir, you did. And I can hardly wait. I got to hand it to you, if you'll pardon me saying it. You're one hell of a cool customer, Frankie."

The one hell of a cool customer was gazing at

that watchtower . . . and feeling a bit warm, to tell the truth.

This whole place . . . the crazy hole in the ground with watertight doors, the underground passage to the large island, a gushing spring lake which was now an Everglades lagoon, exhausted workmen, and gorilla turnkeys . . . a South Seas island paradise with armed guards in a watchtower . . . yeah, this whole place was enough to put an edge on a guy.

But there was nowhere to go, now, but onward.

So, hell, the new project boss of whatever and whomever grabbed his chief gunner by the arm and went onward.

"Changes," he said quietly, "you haven't seen yet, Pip."

11

CRISIS

Incredible as it seemed, these guys had a little Devil's Island operation going here. The rectangular building at the center of the complex, labeled Residence Hall, did combination duty as makeshift barracks, mess hall, lounge, and whatever else a prisoner of war could lay claim to.

Somewhere in the neighborhood of a hundred men were now crowded beneath that roof. They slept on pallets on the floor, which were rolled and stowed against the walls when not in use for sleeping. This was immediately obvious because presently one side of the barracks was wall to wall with sleeping men, the other side serving as a lounge area with its sleep pads in a neat row along the wall while the duty crew sat around in small groups staring blankly at nothing.

Another immediately obvious fact was that the poor bastards wore leg irons twenty-four hours a day and slept chained to the building.

There was no furniture whatever, no partitioning walls, not even for the toilet area or kitchen. The prisoners themselves came in all sizes and descriptions. No uniforms here, either. Each guy was obviously still wearing what he'd brought in on his back—or what was left of it. The lucky ones were those in denims. Their clothing was merely filthy. The others were tattered, as well. Skintones covered the whole range, including an Oriental. There was no equality among the eyes, either. This pair here was hopeless, those over there baffled, another pair, stupefied, this guy, mad as hell.

Good for you, guy. Stay mad as hell. Stay hard.

Bolan knew, now, that he'd been mistaken about the fate of amateurs on a professional's turf—on this turf, anyway. Those devil squads had been aptly named . . . and their interest in amateur smugglers had not been limited to contraband alone. They needed slaves, as well.

A quiet rage was welling deep within Mack Bolan's guts as he surveyed that sorry group. But his comment was cool and in keeping with his role. "Scurvy-looking crew," he said quietly.

The duty turnkey was a barrel-chested youngster with dead eyes and a nasty mouth. "Yeh, well, we break 'em in real quick," he replied, hoisting his "cruncher," a one-inch steel pipe about the length of his arm, and lightly tapping his own skull with it to illustrate the remark.

"I said *scurvy* looking," Bolan growled, throwing a hard look at Papriello. "You know what scurvy is? What kind of food are you giving these people?"

"Beans and rice," said Nasty-Mouth. "All they can hold, twice a day."

"Hold in *what*?" Bolan demanded. "Their *hands*, dammit?"

"Hey, Boss, we feed 'em pretty good," Papriello said quickly. "I mean, if they work good, they eat good. They eat before and after every shift."

"Tell me about those shifts."

"Huh?"

"What's the work routine?"

"Eight on and eight off," Papriello said quietly.

"Eight *what*?"

"Eight *hours*, boss."

"Right around the clock that way? Seven days a week?"

"Right, that's right."

"And they're living on beans and rice?"

Nasty-Mouth had folded his arms across his chest and wisely withdrew from the conversation, looking from one man to the other as the words fired across. Now he ventured an unsought opinion. "Beans has got more protein than meat, I hear."

Bolan said to Papriello, "Oh, great. Julia Childs here is counting their calories." He turned savagely on the turnkey. "You better start counting *vitamins*, dummy! This bunch has all got the *scurvy*! You get some goddamned fresh fruits out here for these people. That shouldn't be a problem! Huh? In Florida? You stock that hole with bags of oranges and bags of grapefruit. And you knock 'em off ten minutes out of every hour and pass around the vitamin C! You hear what I'm saying?"

Papriello came to his boy's rescue. "Boss, hey, it's me at fault. I just didn't come to think about it. I mean, to tell the truth, you know, these people aren't going to be here forever."

"Neither will you," Bolan growled at the Pip. "Not if the goddamned island is rotten with scurvy! You better think about *that*!"

"Jesus, is it contagious?"

"Of course it's contagious!"

Of course it was not. Nor was there any strong probability that the prisoners had been on their beans and rice diet long enough to develop serious vitamin deficiencies. But Bolan had to do something for these people . . . even if he could not do anything for himself. And right now he was merely probing for whatever handle he could find to unwind the thing.

"Jesus, I didn't think."

"That's one of those changes we were talking about!" Bolan told the guy, deciding that the time had arrived for a bit of hard. "You start thinking in the round!"

"Right, right. To tell the truth, I'm very sorry about all this. I mean, after all . . ."

Bolan held a hand toward the turnkey and said, "Give me that damned thing!"

"Sir?"

"The bone breaker! Hand it over!"

The guy surrendered the steel pipe, eyes moving rapidly between the two bosses.

"You don't need this."

"Yessir, pardon me, but I need it."

"Big strong boy like you? For what?"

Papriello explained, "I don't let my boys carry guns around the prisoners. Those guys are dead men, Frankie. They all know they'll never leave this place alive. You can't give guys like that an inch, not an inch. They're dead men already and they know it."

"They're working like dead men, too, aren't they," Bolan said quietly. He tucked the steel pipe under his arm. "Let's get something on the table, here." He made a signal with his eyes and led the two men outside, then said, "You get those god*damned* leg irons off of those people. I mean *forever*. You feed 'em right and you by God treat 'em right. As long as they're alive, let's treat them like men. Maybe then they'll work like men. I've got to tell you, Pip—there's a lot of unhappiness upstairs about the way this job is

97

going. Why do you think I was sent? To make your *boys* happy? Listen, I was sent to make the *company* happy. You guys have got this thing *all* screwed up."

Papriello softly replied, "I tried to get Guido off his ass, Frankie. He just wouldn't take no interest in this thing over here. I tried—"

"To hell with that," Bolan said quietly. "Guido will take his own lumps. That part is over. I don't want to hear about what used to be. I want you to get this damned thing straightened out. Right now."

Papriello turned to the youth and said, "Go take off those chains. All of it. Tell the prisoners there's a new regime around here. Tell 'em things are changing for the better."

"Give 'em some damned *hope*," Bolan suggested.

"We going to give 'em cónjugal visits, too?" sneered Nasty-Mouth.

Bolan whipped the steel pipe around and lightly touched it to the guy's teeth. "One more smart word, guy," he said evenly, "and you'll be gumming beans and rice, yourself, right alongside the others."

The guy paled, muttered something unintelligible, and quickly went inside the building.

Papriello spluttered, "It's getting hard to find good men, Frankie. I guess you know what I mean. Five years ago I wouldn't have let that kid shine my shoes."

"Now you entrust the kingdom to him," Bolan growled.

"What can you do?"

"You stay all the more on your damned toes, that's what you do."

"You're right. You're exactly right."

"Go see that he does it right."

"What? Oh, sure, I . . ."

"It's okay," Bolan said, softening the tone somewhat. "I want to look around some on my own."

"Just give a yell if you need any help."

Bolan smiled. "Who would hear me, eh?"

Papriello smiled back, obviously not exactly understanding the rejoinder but not questioning it, either. He stepped inside the residence hall and Bolan went prowling.

The huts were nicely outfitted, comfortable, self-contained efficiency apartments. Four of them were occupied by sleeping men. Engineers or technicians, no doubt, the brains of the work force. The hut from which Anderson had emerged earlier was set up as an office. It held a small drafting table and the usual office equipment including a copying machine and the inevitable computer terminal plus some exotic communications gear.

Bolan recalled the antennae bristling from the watch tower, deciding that they did not rely upon landline communications in this isolated area, though certainly wires could have been piped through the connecting tunnel.

It required less than a minute to sabotage the radio, via a bare wire laid across a couple of hot circuits in the power supply. The whole thing would arc out the moment power was applied.

But that was just a what-the-hell effort.

The real prize was found in a sheaf of drawings in a drawer of the drafting table. There, in four-color relief, was the whole story of Island X.

And, yes, it was a story to boggle the mind.

Bolan carefully rolled the drawings and encased them in a cardboard tube, placed the tube casually under the arm, and strolled out of there.

Thermal Thursday, indeed. Somehow the subconscious mind had known, even as the day began. And, now, if he could just get off this rock, perhaps the day could be properly concluded.

If . . . yeah.

Carlo the Pip was waiting for him a few paces outside the residence hall, a troubled look playing at the eyes.

"To tell the truth," said the Pip, "maybe I shouldn't bother you with this . . . but then again maybe I should."

"Bother me with what?" Bolan inquired lightly.

"There's a guy inside there, a prisoner, says he wants to talk to you. Says it's very important." Papriello sighed. "Says he knows who you are."

Uh-huh. *If* . . .

"Good for him, send him out here," said

Frankie-Mack with a quiet laugh. "Maybe he can solve my big identity crisis."

But Mack Bolan was not laughing inside. Hell no. A very real identity crisis was close at hand.

12

THE PRISONER

He was a handsome man of about Bolan's age. The eyes were very intelligent, knowing, behind the shaggy beard. Faint traces of a deep Florida tan remained on the muscled flesh. He was barefoot and naked from the waist up. Denim jeans were threadbare in spots and the fly zipper was only half there. Those knowing eyes were tinged with desperation but the guy was struggling to muster some dignity.

Papriello told Bolan, "This is the guy."

"What's his name?" Bolan quietly inquired.

"What's your name, Jack?"

The voice was just a bit choked, not entirely sure of its ground. "My name is William O.

Kessler." He spoke directly to Bolan. "I have something important to talk to you about."

Papriello warned, "This guy has tried every con in the books, Frankie."

"Leave us," Bolan said quietly.

Papriello stood there for a moment, balancing on his toes, then spun about and went back inside.

Bolan placed a hand on the prisoner's shoulder and walked him toward the shoreline. "You wanted to talk, so talk," he prompted.

The man apparently did not know exactly how to start it. He was not all that sure of himself and was evidently searching for a lowkeyed handle. After a moment, he asked, "My name means nothing to you? Kessler? Bill Kessler?"

Bolan quietly replied, "Not right off the top, no."

"Well I'm going to drop a few more on you. If they mean anything to you . . . then maybe you're who I think you are. And maybe you'll know who I am."

"Drop away," Bolan invited casually.

Kessler was watching the Bolan eyes as he carefully enunciated the names. "Bob Wilson . . . Jack Petro . . . Tim Braddock . . . Genghis Conn . . ."

Bolan growled, "That's enough. And you're Bill Kessler."

The guy's hands were beginning to tremble. "You've heard of me, then!"

"No." Bolan gave him a cigarette, lit it, then lit one for himself. "Just trying to fill the inside straight. Why should those names mean something to me?"

They did, of course. They meant a hell of a lot. Each one was the name of a cop who, at one time or another, had figured in Mack Bolan's saga.

"I was hoping they would," Kessler said, choking a bit on the cigarette. "And you did fill that straight, mister."

Very casually, Bolan inquired, "How long you been here?"

"Six weeks, more or less. It's hard to keep a count."

"Would you happen to know a girl called Jean Russell?"

Those desperate eyes blazed with new hope. "God yes! You want a description?"

Bolan asked, "Know the name she was born with?"

Kessler was having a hard time balancing the unaccustomed cigarette smoke with his emotions. Those tortured eyes watered and he fell into a fit of coughing.

They were standing at the waterline of the lagoon. Papriello and Nasty-Mouth were watching them from the porch of the residence hall.

Bolan commanded, "Fall down!" and let the guy have a dummy haymaker.

Kessler fell to the ground and continued

coughing, doubling onto his side in an apparent spasm.

Bolan could hear no sounds from that distant porch but he could clearly see the snicker on Smart-Mouth's face. He told the man on the ground, "Stay there a while. Do you have that name?"

"Fitzpatrick, I believe," Kessler wheezed.

"Close enough," Bolan said, sighing. He took a deep pull at the cigarette and asked, "How'd you get into this mess, guy?"

"I was working undercover. Got taken in a raid over near the Big Cypress."

"Your name is really Kessler?"

"William O., yeah. They don't know I'm a cop. I wouldn't have lasted this long if—"

"Any of the other prisoners know?"

"No."

"Do you have a cadre? Among the prisoners?"

"Sort of. Five other guys. We've been working on an escape plan."

"Reliable men?"

"I think so, yeah."

"What are the prospects for escape?"

"Damned thin. They keep ten men patrolling this hammock. And I guess you've seen the tower. We'd need a boat. We figured—"

"Don't try it," Bolan suggested. "Have you spotted any finks?"

"No finks, no. We're sure of that. These guys are too cocksure, anyway, to bother with finks."

"Okay," Bolan said, sighing. "Well this is going to be a hell of a problem."

"We'll try anything. What can you do?"

"Beats hell out of me, guy. I'm just playing the ear. But I could be the only chance you'll ever get. And I guess today has to be the day. The chief engineer says no more work today. That means all of you will be topside, at least 'til morning. That's the only time we can spring it. You wouldn't want to be in that hole when . . ."

"Whatever you say," Kessler commented eagerly.

"Okay. Whatever comes will be after nightfall. Get your cadre together and very quietly pass the word."

"Nightfall, right."

"You'll have to break quick and clean. No uprising, dammit, no heroics. Just break and run. Get clear. You guys would be the first to die if any overt rescue attempt was made. You know that."

"We've talked about it, yes. But there's no place to run."

"I don't mean forever. I mean find a crack and stay there until the shooting's over."

"We could do that, probably. Now that the damned chains are off."

"Stay clear of that hole, though."

"Right. Uh . . . what do you have in mind?"

"Right now, guy, I've got nothing in mind. You just be ready to break if the excitement starts."

"You mean *when* it starts," Kessler said confidently.

"I mean *if*. At this point, I'm not even sure of my next heartbeat."

Kessler smiled wanly and said, "We'll be praying for you."

"Do that. And, Kessler . . . you don't tell those people *why* they can hope. You don't breathe my name. You can't depend on a desperate man."

"You're depending on me."

"Not really," Bolan said quietly. "Okay. Get up and go back inside. Don't look at me. Just get up and go inside."

Kessler followed the instructions.

A moment later, Bolan was telling Papriello, "He's quite a con artist, yeah."

"What'd he want?"

Bolan chuckled nastily. "Wants to join up."

Papriello chuckled, too. Nasty-Mouth snickered and said, "He's been trying that since the day he got here."

"What'd you tell 'im, Frankie?"

"Told him to drop dead," Bolan growled.

"We caught your sign language," said Nasty-Mouth.

"That was for the con," Bolan explained. "The guy never saw me in his life before. I don't like being conned. You remember that."

Nasty-Mouth sobered quickly, dropping his gaze, and said, "Mr. Cavaretta, I want to apologize for smarting off. Mr. Papriello told me and I swear it was the first I knowed—I mean, I didn't know I was smarting off and I apologize."

"Let those guys take a bath!"

"Sir? They got a—"

"I don't mean that one lousy showerhead for one hundred damn men! God's sake, you got forty jillion barrels of fresh water flowing into this pond every day. Use it. Let 'em swim and lay around in the sun for a while."

Nasty-Mouth replied, "Well, sure, now that the iron is off, I guess why not."

Papriello hastily added his concurrence. "Sure, why not. We'll do that every day from now on. And we're going to get better work out of these guys from now on, too."

"Gives you something to hold over their head," Bolan explained. "No work, no privileges."

"That's exactly right," said the Pip.

"Treat 'em like men," Nasty-Mouth ventured, joining the revolution.

"I'm also going to kill these here death rumors," said Papriello. "Real cool-like, though, you know. We'll pump some hope back into 'em, and a lot better work out of them. Don't you worry none about this joint, Frankie."

Bolan replied, "I haven't got a worry in the world, Pip."

But he did. Oh yeah, he did.

He had the secret of Island X under his arm and the lives of a hundred doomed men in his hands. And even the master con artist of them all had plenty to worry about.

13

STAYING STRAIGHT

Mack Bolan had never been the sort of man who had trouble making decisions. Which is not to say that he did not carefully weigh all the various alternatives and options present in a given situation. But he did not agonize the decision process; once all the variables had been considered, it was characteristic that he moved immediately along the most realistic route toward his goal.

At the moment, he was moving quickly and surely along the route of disengagement from the forces of Lucifer's Ladder. Already he had overstayed and overplayed the masquerade. A penetration of this nature could work for a while —if a guy really knew what he was at—but all the expertise and artistry in the world could not prevent the thing from falling apart under external influences—such as a phone call from someone higher up, or any one of a hundred other possibilities.

So he was putting that joint behind him. There was nothing to be gained and everything to lose by overstaying, now that he had the answers to that place. As for Bill Kessler and his Doomed One Hundred, there seemed to be no particular urgency to that situation; it would keep until a reasonably safe and sure rescue could be developed.

Bolan walked with Papriello across the Level I catwalk without so much as a glance at the busy men inside the glass cubicle. Some other hardhats were pounding steel far below and the compressors were still sucking and banging. Papriello rolled his eyes as a comment to the ear-shattering noise and signaled an invitation for Bolan to precede him to the monorail.

"Why don't you drive it back," he shouted, his voice barely audible above the din. "It's very simple. You just got the one control. Cycle it over to 'local' and hold it there. It's a dead man's throttle there, see. All you do is throw it—yeah, over there—throw it to 'local' and hold it there. When we get off at the other end, you let go and she's back on 'remote.' That's so the car can be called from either end. Like an elevator, see. Only it's dummy proofed, so you can't forget and leave it in local control."

Bolan growled his understanding and sent the car back to Santelli Island. He knew that Papriello was curious about the mailing tube he'd brought from Anderson's office but the guy would have died before inquiring about it. Mob traditions simply did not allow such questions. Bolan would not have had to volunteer any information whatever, but he did not want the guy's mind sticking to any minor worries. Also, that roll of drawings was Bolan's ticket out of that joint.

As they ascended the stairwell to the surface, he lightly tapped the cylinder against the Pip's shoulder and told him, "You didn't see me with this. Right?"

The guy grinned and replied, "Right."

"I've got to take it to Miami. They want to see it."

"Oh yeah, sure, I understand."

But obviously the Pip understood very little.

"I'll try to get it back before the Doc misses it. But if he misses it then he misses it. They still want to see it. And if Doc don't like it, then that's just too damn bad."

The guy was getting it, now.

"Oh right, right. To tell the truth, I never liked this idea of him reporting direct. He could be telling 'em anything and how would I know?

112

Hell, I never know what the guy is telling 'em. For damn sure, Guido never knew."

"He'll never know, now," Bolan said, lifting an eyebrow to emphasize the remark.

"I see what you mean. Poor Guido. But it's his own damn fault. I tried to keep the guy . . ."

They'd reached the trap door to the portal. Bolan placed a hand on Papriello's arm and said, "Before we go up there, Pip . . ."

"Yeah?"

"I could have told you this as soon as I got here. But I had to wait. You know why I had to wait."

"Tell me what, Frankie?"

"I didn't come here to take over from Guido."

"No?"

"No. You must know why I came. Hey, you know. And why I couldn't tell you 'til now."

A grin was beginning to spread across the face of the gunner so long denied his own desk. . . "You mean . . . ?"

"I had to check you out, Pip. Standard procedure. I had to do that."

"Jesus, Frankie. That's okay. You check me out any damn time you please."

"You're the boss here, now."

"Jesus! I just don't know what to say! I'm speechless!"

Bolan chuckled as he told the gloating gunner, "You're long overdue. You know that. You've earned it."

"I'll try to keep on earning it, Frankie. Jesus!

Tell them—tell the men—well, I'm grateful. I'll give 'em a hundred percent all the time."

Bolan grinned. "Make it a hundred and ten."

The guy was stunned. Obviously this was the last news he'd ever expected to hear. He could not keep his mouth straight. "Right, right. You know I will.'"

"Starting at midnight."

"Huh?"

"We turn the book at midnight. Just to keep it all straight."

The guy was becoming confused again. "Keep what straight, Frankie?"

"The counts, the split. You know. Hey, Carlo. You got to get used to high finance."

From the grin on Papriello's beaming face, he was already getting used to it. Nor had he missed the subtle shift of respect which called him "Carlo" instead of "Pip."

Bolan felt no particular sympathy nor enmity for the guy. Let him have a few hours of imagined glory. It would all turn to ashes by nightfall, anyway, if Bolan had his final way with this group. Nor was he simply having fun at Papriello's expense. There was a studied effect implicit in every movement of the Bolan mind . . . and mouth.

"I think it deserves a celebration," he said as they moved into the barren room at the surface. "I think it calls for a party."

Papriello was beaming at Vesperanza, keeper

of the portal, and the big legbreaker was grinning back without knowing why.

"We gonna get some broads, Pip?"

"You're gonna get more than that, Rock," Papriello replied gaily. He flicked dancing eyes at Bolan and asked, "Can I tell 'im, Frankie?"

"Why not? He can be the first to know."

"How many broads," asked the gorilla, almost drooling in anticipation of the good news.

"Broads, broads, that's all he's got on his mind, Frankie," Papriello said in mock disgust. "To tell the truth, I think his nose bleeds every month. I'm not telling that guy nothing. I'll save it for someone who cares."

"Aw shit, now, Pip."

Bolan told the big bruiser, "You better get used to calling him mister. I would if I was you. I'd call him mister."

"Why?"

"Figure it out."

But Vesperanza already had it figured out. The broad face sobered and turned mean. Very briefly mean. But Bolan took note of the quick transition from glad through bad to sad. "Couldn't happen to a better man," said the keeper of the portal in a melancholy voice. "It's too late for me, I guess. But I'm happy for you, Mr. Papriello. God, pardon me, but that sounds funny. Mr. Papriello. So what does it mean? To me, I mean? Who's doing what?"

"Guido's out and Carlo's in, that's what it

means," Bolan soberly informed him. "But now you listen to this and you mark it at the top of your head. Nobody goes across 'till Carlo says so. Nobody. The portal is closed."

"It's closed, right. Why?"

"You don't need to know why," Papriello replied for Bolan.

"And nobody comes the other way," Bolan said sternly.

"Okay, it's closed both ways. And I don't need to know why."

"That's right," said Papriello.

"But is tonight still the night?" Vesperanza inquired anxiously.

Papriello burst out laughing.

Bolan chuckled and said, "Count on it, Rocky. Tonight *is* the night. How many will you need?"

"Four or five would do," the guy replied, grinning. "For starters."

"You guys figure it out between yourselves," Bolan said. He patted his pockets. "I left my damn lighter somewhere. Maybe it fell out down below. I bet it's in the tunnel of love—on the damn seat, maybe."

"The Rock can run down and get it for you, Frankie."

"Naw, naw, I better go myself. That lighter was gave to me by old man Castiglione himself. I better . . ."

He was still mumbling to himself as he opened the trap and went below.

Bolan would not have returned to that hole for all the cigarette lighters in Florida. But he had to get back down there. He popped open the control panel for the monorail car and used his penlight to study the logic circuits. It was a simple fix. Pop-out connectors had been utilized in the wiring. He popped one loose from a vital circuit then carefully restored the panel cover. Dummy-proof or not, that car would not now respond to a call from the other end.

"I found it," he said, showing the mafiosi his lighter as he rejoined them. "God, I would've hated to lose it."

"Hey, that's great," said Papriello. "Listen, Frankie, I made a decision. I'm making Rock my number one cock around here. I'm hoping you'll second the motion."

"You couldn't have picked a better man," Bolan agreed soberly. "But let's keep it like it is for today. You know what I mean."

No, Papriello did not know what Bolan meant. But he grinned and said, "Exactly what I had in mind. Rock—we're both depending on you to keep this portal closed. Until I say different."

"Hey, it is closed," Vesperanza assured one and all. "And you can just send those broads in here to help me keep it closed, when they get here."

The two "bosses" went into the sunlight laughing.

"I had to do that," Papriello explained, sobering quickly as soon as they were clear of the shack. "Rock has been around a long time. He's deserving, too."

"You did the right thing," Bolan assured him.

"Ah, hell, Frankie, it's a beautiful day. I can't believe how down I was when that sun came up this morning. And how high I am now. It's like a dream. Say, don't pinch me. I don't wanta know."

Bolan was not about to pinch him. Not right now, anyway. That would come later.

The sun was at the midday zenith. Thermal Thursday, at midpoint. And the surface had barely been scratched.

"I want you to go see if my plane is back," Bolan told the beautiful dreamer. "I'm going to the house and get my stuff together. Tell Grimaldi I want to take off in twenty minutes. Hell, this is great. I figured to be out here all day, at least. I brought enough clothes to last a week. Listen, I have to tell you this, Carlo. You really have things in good control here. I made a lot of sounds but that's all it was. I had to do it. I hope you understand that. But I'm going to Miami to tell those men that Santelli Island is in the best of hands. I wanted you to know that. And, uh, that other stuff—you know, the prisoner problem, that's just between you'n me. Okay? I don't need to say anything about that, do I?"

"Christ, no. Frankie . . . what can I say? Hey, you're the very greatest. I'm sorry you have to leave so soon. Hey, really, I hate to see you go. But I understand. Hey, I understand."

The guy was thrilled to death that Bolan was leaving.

Bolan said, "My gal will see to the, uh, social diversions for your boys. We'll take care of all that soon as we hit Miami. Believe it, you'll get the very highest grade beef around. Depend on Jeanie for that. And I meant what I said about that celebration. You deserve it."

"Why'd we close the portal?"

Bolan tapped the guy again with the cylinder of drawings. "Just why do you think I'm taking this stuff to Miami?"

"I don't even know what it is you're taking to Miami, Frankie."

"Right. And all you got to know, Carlo, is that I want that portal shut tight until we've had a chance to examine this stuff very closely in Miami."

"Oh, you mean . . . you don't want those hardhats . . ."

"I want them to stay put, right."

"They'll stay put, count on it."

"That's exactly what I'm counting on. Now you better go see about the plane. I need to get moving."

"Right, I'll go see. God, it's been a pleasure having you here, Frankie. You'll, uh, let me know about the hardhats. We need to rotate the duty shift at five o'clock."

"Not today, Carlo."

"Oh. I see. Okay. Uh, like I said, it's been a real pleasure."

But the pleasure was all Bolan's. And he was more than pleased to share some of it with Jean Kirkpatrick Russell. "Game's over," he told her as he stepped into her room. "Get ready, we're going home."

"I believe you're forgetting a promise you made to me," she said, eyeing him curiously. "Or are you?"

"Maybe not," he replied. "Not if you came out here looking for Bill Kessler."

Oh, indeed she had.

She had, indeed.

Now she would be going home without her Bill. But her mere presence here had lent credibility to a daring masquerade and her value to the Bolan game, thus far, was inestimable. Bolan owed her one. And, dammit, he intended to deliver.

14

TURNING POINT

Brognola had moved his task force deep into the Everglades to within a few miles of Santelli Island, the force consisting of a collection of large, wheeled vehicles, two small helicopters, and several trailer-transported speed boats. It was quite a convoy but well disguised as an EPA group, with each of the vehicles appropriately marked.

He'd also sent a helicopter to pick up the archeologist, Louis Cardinez, and an associate named Washburn, a geologist. Cardinez brought along some rough artwork he'd done years earlier on the Satan's Hammock phenomenon and seemed entirely pleased to be taken into the police adventure now descending upon that "old dig" of his.

Washburn, on the other hand, seemed a bit nervous and uncertain of his role in all this. Both men were fully cooperative, however, and obviously anxious to help in the investigation.

One of the sketches brought by Cardinez looked like a bottom-heavy, severely unbalanced hourglass. The top part was a relatively shallow bowl-shaped object with gently sloping sides pulling toward a slender "neck" at its base. The bottom part was more bell-shaped, several times longer than the upper bowl, and considerably wider at the base than the "top" of the upper chamber.

"What you are seeing, here," the archeologist explained, "represents a rather phenomenal development of an otherwise common occurrence in this particular part of the country. The lower part is, in simple terms, a spring. Simply a spring. This part of the country literally abounds with fresh water springs, which are largely responsible for the great proliferation of lakes in the region. Where Satan's Hammock takes its departure from the ordinary spring-fed lake is found in this huge vertical cavern which underlies the lake basin. Please understand . . . the lake did not produce the cavern. Quite the opposite, the cavern—or, more precisely, the water flowing up through the cavern—produced the lake."

Brognola ran a finger across the "neck" of the

122

hourglass as he asked, "This was the original land surface?"

"Still is," interposed Washburn, the geologist. "A certain degree of sedimentation has occurred, naturally, but this sinkhole occurred in modern times. Within the past few hundred years."

"Sinkhole?"

"A collapse sinkhole, yes. They're fairly common in *karst* terrain. The entire Ocala plain is *karst*. They—"

Brognola interrupted to say, "Wait a minute, you're going technical on me. What is *karst?*"

"It's simply a term used to describe certain evolutionary features produced by solution channels and caves in underlying bedrock. Typically, in *karst* topography, you have surface water running off underground instead of via your usual surface streams and rivers. The Florida *karst* is more or less unique. It's a situation where you have flat-lying bedrock of limestone at just about sea level. Surface-water runoff from distant elevations enters the limestone flats and goes underground, producing solution conduits which can become quite large. In other words, underground streams and rivers."

"And where do they go? Those underground streams?"

"Typically they will discharge offshore as submarine springs of fresh water, at some point where the limestone interfaces with nonporous rock. Or they can bubble up as springs at most any point where surface limestone is present."

The geologist tapped Cardinez's sketch. "Such as here. This particular formation is rightly termed a *cenote*, which is a bottle-shaped collapse sinkhole. At Satan's Hammock, the limestone bedrock is only very thinly covered with soil. Various factors contributed, at that point, to produce a surface dome—that is, a large vertical cavern whose dome continued expanding through the ages until it broke through the surface."

"But filled with water," Brognola said.

"Oh yes. It is the scouring action of the water which produces the cavity. Had the water level dropped at some point, say, five hundred years ago, then the cavity would not have been allowed to expand to the surface elevation. And we would never have learned of the formation. Unless, of course, someone began mining operations hereabouts. Many subterranean formations are discovered in that manner."

Brognola scratched his nose and commented, "You're saying that there could be entire networks of formations like this that we'd never know about."

"I'm saying that there *are*."

"Uh huh." Brognola thoughtfully pulled at his nose. "Well tell me, gentlemen—what the hell *good* is something like this?"

Washburn only grinned at his response to the question.

After a moment, Cardinez replied, "It's a dynamic planet, Mr. Brognola."

"No, I mean from the human standpoint. Let me correct that: from the *greed* standpoint. What good is it?"

Washburn said, "If I owned that land, I'd put glass-bottom boats on the lake for the casual tourist and rent scuba gear for the diving enthusiasts. It's a wonderland down there. And the water is crystal clear."

"Think like a *hood*, though," Brognola persisted.

"You mean, some illegal use," Cardinez said drily.

"With great profit potentials, yes."

The archeologist replied, "If you're thinking of buried treasure or some such nonsense, forget it. Natural wonders you will find in those waters, yes, but that is all. I agree with Washburn. It would make a tremendous tourist attraction. But God, it would cost a fortune to develop it. Now, you could think along those lines. And I believe it would be a relatively safe investment. Over the long run, the return should be quite respectable."

"I'm talking about disrespectful people," Brognola grunted.

Washburn said, "Are we talking about things like organized crime?"

"Yeah."

"Well it has been common knowledge for years that organized crime elements are fairly well entrenched in this state. And I understand that they sometimes diversify into legitimate business ventures. This would be an excellent way to invest ill-gotten gains."

Brognola growled, "Maybe so."

It was at this point that the prodical son returned. A marshal poked his head into the vehicle, caught Brognola's eye, and mouthed a single inaudible word: "Striker."

The head fed excused himself and went outside.

A Ford Mustang had penetrated the circle of official vehicles and was parked in the shadow of Bolan's fabulous warwagon, the GMC motorhome which the guy had converted into a rolling dreadnought.

Jack Grimaldi was behind the wheel of the Mustang, jawing easily with a marshal who was leaning into the open window.

Brognola paused for a quick word with the pilot. "Is he okay?"

"That guy? Hell, he's in better shape than I am. And all I've done is sit and wait."

Brognola squeezed the pilot's hand and went into the motorhome. He should have knocked before entering. Striker and Brognola's star female recruit were wrapped up in an impassioned embrace just inside the hatch.

The head fed *harrumphed* and squeezed past the couple to take a seat in the war room.

"Any time you're ready, people," he said quietly, after a moment.

April came out of the clinch with dancing eyes and a scarlet face. Striker took a moment to compose himself. He lit a cigarette then took the girl by the hand and steered her to a seat. Then he grinned and shook Brognola's hand.

There had been, yeah, a brief tension there. It was a normal characteristic of the strange relationship between the two men. Stout friends from almost the beginning   but a persistently strained friendship. Brognola understood the nature of the strain. Between people of such diverse paths, the strain went with the territory.

"How'd it go?" he casually asked the big guy.

"It went okay," said Striker in characteristic understatement. "Do you have Riappi?"

Brognola nodded solemnly. "Kicking and screaming about his constitutional rights, but we've got him. He's in the club van."

The club van was a jailhouse on wheels.

The Striker grinned and said, "Wants to be charged, eh?"

"Yeah."

"For starters, then, hit him with kidnapping and illegal detention."

"That's what he wants to hit *me* with," Brognola growled humorously. "Who'd he kidnap?"

"One William O. Kessler and about a hundred John Does. His devil crews have been taking prisoners for slave labor. Kessler happens to be a cop. He could make your case. And that's just for starters."

"What the hell is going on, Striker?" Brognola asked soberly. "What's all this devil's island stuff?"

Bolan smiled solemnly and reached behind Brognola to produce a fat cardboard tube. He withdrew from it a roll of engineering drawings and spread them on the floor at Brognola's feet. From the top drawing, the chief fed instantly recognized the lopsided hourglass sketched by Cardinez but this one was much more professionally drawn, much more involved, and minutely detailed.

"Son of a bitch," Brognola breathed, forgetting himself in front of the lady. "What the hell are they *doing* out there?"

Bolan fanned the drawings and selected one from the center of the stack. "Take a look at this," he said, "then ask what they're doing."

But Brognola could not ask.

He could not immediately believe, even.

Nor could Bolan, obviously.

"What do you make of it?" Brognola asked the big guy, after a silent study of the incredible evidence.

"That's for a better head than mine to say," Bolan replied quietly. "I'm just a soldier. But I'd have to call it foreign relations."

So would Brognola. But, like Bolan, he'd like to refer the matter to better heads. "Someone I want you to meet," he muttered. "Put on some dark glasses or something. We're taking this to a higher court."

"It will have to be a quick trip," Bolan warned. "I've got a fire mission and it won't keep."

128

But it would.

If this evidence meant what it seemed to mean, anything else would keep . . . indefinitely. Any damned thing else.

15

EXPERT OPINION

If one could believe the evidence, it appeared that the engineers at Satan's Hammock were working on a network of subterranean conduits which extended well beyond the North American mainland to incredible distances.

Three major routes had been painstakingly mapped on an oceanographic chart of the region. The shortest of these angled off in a generally easterly direction to pass beneath Biscayne Bay, just south of Miami, terminating near Andros Island on the Great Bahama Bank.

Another proceeded due south from Satan's Hammock, running beneath Everglade's National Park and Florida Bay, passing the Keys of

Islamorada and continuing through Cuba to a terminus at the island of Jamaica in the Caribbean.

The third branched off from the Jamaican conduit just north of Havana to proceed westerly along offshore Cuba to a point on the Yucatan Peninsula of Mexico.

The three routes were marked, perhaps facetiously, "Bahama Boulevard," "Jamaica Drive," and "Yucatan Avenue."

"It is not as incredible as it may seem," said the geologist. "The flat limestone bedrock which forms the spine of Florida extends well into the Greater Antilles. In fact, you could think of it as a single, continuous platform upon which nature has constructed the entire peninsula of Florida and most of the islands between here and Venezuela."

"What do you mean by *platform?*" Brognola inquired, rather irritably. "I've never really studied geology but it has always been my understanding that the continents and the seabeds are different animals entirely."

Washburn smiled faintly as he replied, "I have spent my entire life in the study of geology, Mr. Brognola, and I discover new marvels every day. Certainly there is no way to condense a lifetime study into a few simple phrases which will give you the same understanding that I have. But let me assure you that the phenomena which you are now contemplating are usually associated with the laying down of limestone. Now limestones of this nature are relatively modern rocks, in the geological sense. They are formed principally by complex interactions between biological organisms and sand. What is now the peninsula of Florida was, in recent geological time, a shallow sea separating the Gulf of Mexico from the Atlantic Ocean. Deposition of tiny biological debris upon the sands of this shallow sea formed the limestone bedrock. I'm putting this very generally, very roughly, understand, for the sake of brevity. But over the eons a skeletal structure of bedrock was formed, upon which was later impressed the soils and other detritus from the Appalachians. The final result is the state of Florida as we know it today. But, now, ocean currents played a large role in that formation. Although the supporting bedrock extends for hundreds of miles below the Straits of Florida, the natural currents discouraged the landbuilding processes at that point. What then occurred beyond the Straits of Florida can be seen as a discontinuous process which resulted in the island chains of the Antilles. At one time, I may add, Florida itself was such a discontinuous chain of small islands. Which is why I say that you could view the entire development as being mounted upon a single platform."

During that discourse, Bolan had been studying the oceanographic map upon which the routes had been traced. And he now had a question for the geologist. "Are we talking about the continental shelf?"

"In this particular area, yes, more or less."
The geologist traced the outline on the map
with his finger. "You will note that the shelf is
virtually continuous between North and South
America. Politically they may be two continents.
Geologically, they are one. And it should be
fairly obvious that at one time the north coast of
Venezuela was fitted rather snugly to North
America in what is now called the Gulf of Mexico. The important element, however, for this
discussion, lies in the grand circle of islands
called the West Indies, which forms the eastern
boundary of the Caribbean Sea—and which are
actually vestigial remnants of what was once
the eastern shelf of the supercontinent, America,
in those latitudes."

Bolan said, "So the Yucatan connection is
valid, also."

Washburn replied, "Understand, I am not
certifying as to the validity of any of this. I am
merely providing the expert opinion as to the
possibility that these conduits *could* exist. But I
am not an oceanographer and I have not kept
abreast of the many burgeoning studies now
being conducted in these areas. If you will look
at the sea chart, however, you will note that the
Yucatan Channel separating Cuba from the
eastern prominence of Yucatan is shown as a
rather chaotic area. There are both trenches and
rises in that channel. But very shallow water
covers much of the Yucatan offshore zones. I
would be not at all surprised to learn that a con-

133

tinuous limestone shelf underlies the Yucatan Channel."

"Good lord!" Brognola exploded. "This just blows too damned much of the mind! Do you people realize that we are talking about hundreds upon hundreds of miles of . . . of . . ."

Washburn quietly said, "Roughly five hundred miles to Jamaica, yes, as the crow flies."

"But that's ridiculous! Five hundred damned miles of caves? I've never . . . this is just . . ."

Cardinez thoughtfully stroked his chin and told the sputtering official, "The wonders of man have nowhere begun to approach the natural wonders of our environment. We speak of the solid earth and all that mechanistic nonsense but the hard truth is that we occupy a phenomenal and dynamic planet which the puny hand of man could never subdue. I was thinking . . ." He angled a sidewise glance at the geologist. "Who was that fellow, George?—came down a few years ago from—remember, he'd been researching the New River Cave in Virginia?"

Washburn replied, "The speleologist, you mean. Cave hydrology was his specialty, wasn't it?"

"I believe so, yes. Now why can't I think of his name? Had all these passionate ideas about continental linkage via water dynamics." The archeologist fixed Brognola with a thoughtful stare. "This is the expert you should be talking to. Fellow spent several months on our campus thoroughly researching every scrap of information on peninsular dynamics." He turned back to the geologist. "Was it Williams?—Williamson?"

"Something like that, yes. Come to think of it, wasn't he interested in Satan's Hammock?"

"Oh yes, and all of our underground phenomena. A very curious fellow, not too socially minded, forever had his nose buried in a—"

Bolan interrupted, "Man in his early fifties?—stocky build, red face?"

"Why yes, I . . ."

Bolan sighed. "The name is Anderson."

"Yes! Paul Anderson. You've already spoken to him, then."

"But not nearly enough," Bolan replied stonily. He signaled Brognola with the eyes and huddled with him out of earshot from the others. "Anderson's our man," he reported quietly. "He's running that show, over there. And he has direct linkage with the Santelli headshed."

"Then it's for real," Brognola replied worriedly. "How the hell do you read this, Striker? What do they hope to gain from all this?"

"Let's talk some more with the experts," Bolan suggested. He returned to the conference table and reshuffled the drawings, placing the "hell hole" artwork on the top of the stack. It was a cross-sectional representation of the caverns at Satan's Hammock, appropriately colored to distinguish between air chambers and water chambers.

"This really is remarkable," said Cardinez,

eyeing the drawing. "I have been there many times. I knew that horizontal cavities existed near the base of the cenote and I suspected the presence of other large chambers . . . but I had no idea that anything such as this . . ."

The drawing depicted the two primary chambers side by side. The north chamber was the dry hole, in which the construction was taking place. The south chamber was the water-filled cavern underlying the lake. In cross-section, many horizontal conduits traversed the site at various levels and in varying sizes. Several of the larger conduits were represented as passing directly through the dry chamber.

"You can see what they've done, here," said Washburn, indicating several points on the drawing. "Initially both chambers were water-filled. They've established a diversion system and pumped the water out of the north chamber. In effect, what we have here, now, is a viable portal into an underground river. It looks like a workable system."

"What do you mean by a *viable portal*?" Brognola asked.

"Think of it as an underground riverport," Washburn explained. "What they are constructing down there is the rough equivalent of a lock and dam system. They are establishing ingress/egress for an underground river."

"Now wait a minute," said the head fed, the voice once again edging into an incredulous register. "I thought we were talking about *caves*. Now you're saying underground *rivers*."

"We've been saying it all along," Washburn said drily. "Sorry, I thought you understood that. That is what is represented on the oceanographic map we were just studying."

Very quietly, Bolan said, "But don't leap to any early conclusions, Hal." He was thinking of the monorail tunnel linking the two islands but did not wish to mention it publicly. "If those guys are pumping water, then they could be building a four-lane highway down there, for all we know."

But Washburn vigorously shook his head in negation of that idea. "I strongly doubt that. If the mapping is accurate—that is, if it is a valid trace—then it would suggest the presence of deep-lying continuous faults traversing the entire length of the limestone shelf, through which surface water is being abducted from the North American continent to rises at the southern extremities. And if this pictograph is accurate . . ." he thumbed the cross-sectional, ". . . then I would have to say that these solution conduits—which would follow the fault lines—are quite sizeable and are no doubt moving huge volumes of water."

"Wouldn't there be seasonal variations?" Bolan asked, recalling something that Pip the Boss had told him.

"To a degree, yes. And the flow could be controlled, to a degree, by this magnificent installation they're putting in there . . . but . . . highways beneath the Caribbean? I doubt that."

Bolan thought about it for a moment then said, "Doctor Washburn, I've been in that hole. These doors . . ." he tapped the drawing with a finger, ". . . are larger than this trailer. As a rough estimate, I'd say they are at least twenty-five feet in diameter. Some of them may be larger than that. Considering a channel of water that large, and assuming that the entire channel —pardon me, you called it a conduit—assuming that the conduit is running at full capacity, wouldn't it be a hell of an engineering feat to shut that flow down?"

"Absolutely," Washburn smiled soberly. "And despite what my distinguished colleague here may have to say about the matter, the puny hand of man has indeed gone a long way toward subduing the rampaging wonders of nature. It could be done. It *has* been done."

"It still sounds like baloney to me," opined Brognola.

The grinning geologist said, "That's what they said about Hoover Dam . . . and Aswan and all the others . . . *before* they were built."

"Yeah," Brognola *harrumphed,* ". . . but an underground river. Anyway, how would they know where those damned things come out? And just because they're twenty-five feet across at Satan's Hammock doesn't mean they stay that big."

"That's right," Washburn said. "But if you will look at the oceanographic study, the routes traced indicate a more or less constant dimension except for zones of considerable temporary expansion."

"But how could they know that?" Brognola growled.

"Perhaps through physical exploration."

Cardinez laughed nervously. "Not by one such as I," he said.

Bolan suggested, "But maybe by someone with passionate interest?"

"Such as Paul Anderson," Washburn said quietly.

"Yeah," Bolan said.

"It's possible, of course. But there are other methods for tracing lost rivers. We usually use dyes or radioactive tracers."

"But that wouldn't tell you much about subterranean dimensions," Bolan suggested.

"Not really, no. Which is why I raised the possibility of a physical exploration. See here, with solution conduits in Floridian *karst,* the gradients are usually very slight and the conduits themselves quite sizeable. By gradients I mean the degree of slope. Assuming that the darned thing does not end in a rabbit hole at the edge of the continental shelf a mile below sea level, it could be quite an exhilarating exploration."

"And," Bolan said, expanding the idea, "if it ends on dry land or in a situation similar to the

139

one at Satan's Hammock, then you've got yourself a secret passageway beneath the sea."

"That's it exactly. And I believe that's exactly what old Anderson has found, here."

Bolan asked, "How long ago was it you said this guy was on your campus?"

Washburn glanced at Cardinez and said, "Oh, several years ago. Wasn't it?"

The archeologist nodded solemnly as he replied, "At least two years ago, maybe three. I could look it up."

"Two years or three," Bolan said, "it really doesn't matter. There's been plenty of time for the guy to work this thing." He again pulled Brognola aside and told him, "This is out of my league, Hal. It's your problem. My problem is out there on that hammock. There are a hundred men out there who—"

"Well wait a damned minute!" Brognola hissed. "It's all the same damned problem. This damned thing has heinous possibilities. My God, it could be a national security matter! I have to take this upstairs."

"While you're doing that," Bolan pointed out, "the Muscatel group is going to discover that they've been waltzed around by an imposter. That's going to make them very nervous—and probably the first thing they will do is destroy all the living evidence. That means a hundred doomed men. I can't wait for you to take it upstairs, Hal."

The chief fed was in a hell of a sweat.

But he knew that Bolan spoke the truth.

He replied, finally, "Okay. It's your game. We'll do it your way. First things first, and we'll pick up the pieces later. How do I support you?"

"You should move immediately on the Muscatel group. But do it quietly. I want no shock waves reaching Santelli Island ahead of me. Then—"

"You've said it several times now, and I don't know who you're talking about. What is this Muscatel group?"

"Santelli and company. I think you'll find it's the remnants of the old Castiglione family, holed up and holding forth in Miami. There's a place over on the Gold Coast called Muscatel's. It's a private residence club. That's where Riappi was headed when you intercepted him."

"Okay, I'm reading you. We can handle that end of things, no sweat. But what about you? You can't storm that island all alone."

Bolan smiled soberly and asked, "Why the hell not?"

Brognola stared at his friend through a moment of strained silence then quietly replied, "Well maybe you can, at that."

Yeah. Maybe he could, at that. But, this time, he would not be entirely alone.

16

OPTIONS

It was good to be in the warwagon again. And it was especially good to have April Rose at his side. He angled a soft gaze her way and quietly asked, "Lost your edge?"

She answered with an impish smile. "If I have, I know a good way to sharpen it up. Park this rig, soldier, and we'll discuss it."

"Shameless," he said. "Brazen."

"Male chauvinist coward," she replied quickly.

"I've missed you, April."

"Thank God," she said, sighing. "Myself, I've only been climbing the walls. Don't you *ever* go off and leave me again."

"I needed the time," he told her.

"I know." She sighed again. "So what did you decide?"

He shrugged his shoulders. "It seems that the decisions have been made for me," he replied quietly.

"That's pure bull," she said, without emotion. "We make our own decisions and you know it."

He told her, "I didn't decide to be a man, April. You didn't decide to be a woman. You were born that way and I was born this way. Within that limited framework, okay, sure, I decided to wear pants and stand up when I pee. And I decided to put on a uniform and go to war. But the options have always been very narrow, haven't they? They still are."

She said, "Maybe."

"Maybe, hell. They always are. And the more important the decision, the tighter the options."

"I suppose that's true, when you look at it that way."

"Uh huh. The most important decisions are made in childhood, I think. They frame the process and load the ballot box. What comes after that is more or less conditioned reflex. We are decent or we are not. We are brave or we are not. The important decisions have all been made. By a child."

She said, "My God. No wonder the world is in such a mess, if that's true."

"I believe it's true," he quietly assured her.

After a moment, she said, "You may have something there, soldier." She was trying to keep it light. "So little Mackie Bolan decided to go to Washington and help the prezzydint."

Bolan chuckled and replied, "Something like that, yeah."

"Well, I'm glad. Although I don't know why. I think they're suckering you, soldier. You've just about got this damned lousy war won. And before you can even raise the eyes and proclaim your victory, they're dragging you off to another one. But I'm still glad. Because I believe what General MacArthur said. Old soldiers never die. And I sure don't want to see you simply fade away, old boy. I want to *help* you there. In a warm bed. Please! Mack, dammit, please stop this damned bus and take me to bed!"

He growled, "Hey, hey."

Tears were erupting and beginning to stream down those glistening cheeks. "I'm kidding, of course. Just kidding. My arms don't really ache for you. My belly isn't knotted in desire. I just want to see you get out there and *kill* 'em, killer. I just want to see you straighten out this wacky world. All alone, all by yourself, the only damn guy in the world with a holy mission. I'll put flowers on your grave, young soldier, and I'll see that your tombstone is suitably inscribed. Here lies little Mackie Bolan. He decided at the age of seven to die with his combat boots on."

He said, "God's sake, April. What happened to your hard?"

"I'm sorry." She swiped angrily at the tears.

144

"You said it, guy. I didn't decide to be a woman. It was my misfortune to be born this way."

"You don't look all that unfortunate to me," he said, sweeping her with the eyes. He kissed his palm and folded it up, making a fist and offering it to her. "Save this 'til after the battle. See how much interest it builds, compounded on the heartbeat. And we'll look into the unfortunate circumstances of your birth."

She laughed through her tears and took the big fist in both dainty hands, raised it to her lips, kissed it. "Damn, I'm getting hard," she sighed, wriggling uncomfortably against the seat.

"Wrong edge, kid," he said, laughing with her.

"Hard is hard," she replied. "Any old edge will do."

"I'm going to need both edges," he reminded her. "The combat hard, first. You'd better radio check Grimaldi."

Yeah. Time was running out. But all the careful preparations had been made, all the options considered, nightfall was mere minutes away, and the land bridge to Santelli Island was dead ahead.

Dead ahead, yeah.

Grimaldi had been sent ahead on a high scouting mission, using one of Brognola's helicopters.

"Tell the Sarge they're on the doubledamn hard," he reported to April. "They're running back and forth between the islands in swamp buggies and I can see patrols everywhere. Also a big car is now streaking toward the north side, I'd say headed toward the bridge. Tell him it's a no-go, repeat, no-go."

Bolan took the mike from April to reply, "Good work, flyboy. But it's too late to abort. Request you stand by to assist but only upon direct request. Play it cool, buddy, play it damn cool."

"There ain't no cool out here, buddy. Not where you're headed."

So what the hell? It was Thursday, wasn't it? And all the options had been used. *This* lousy war was not won yet, April.

Bolan swung the command console toward April's position and told her, "Raise and lock for the fire."

"What's the target?" she asked crisply, all business and all hard edge like the flip of a switch.

"Dead ahead," he replied. "Straight down the pike. We'll probably have to punch our way off this bridge."

"Punch off, aye," she said. "Platform is raised . . . platform is locked . . . I have a Firing Go."

Yeah . . . the time had run out . . . and all the options had been used.

Now it was nothing but the fire ahead.

—

17

NIGHTFALL

The black limousine was pulled broadside across the road, blocking the exit from the bridge which itself was no more than a narrow roadway built atop a connecting landfill. Human figures were scurrying about behind that vehicle and the first *zoom* of the optics centered upon a double-barreled shotgun using the rooftop of the limousine as a gun rest.

Though the daylight was rapidly dwindling under the descending mantle of nightfall, the optics resolution focused clearly on the scowling visage behind that shotgun: it was old reliable, nothing more and nothing less Johnny Paoli, he of the dimwit but determined disposition.

Bolan could almost hear the guy ticking off the instructions on his fingertips: block the damn bridge, right; don't let nobody in, right; whack off that damn Frankie's head if he shows up, right.

Huh-uh, not right.

It was one of those unfortunate situations where all the rights added up to a deadly wrong. Even for Mack Bolan, yeah. He took no satisfaction in the destruction of such a man.

The warwagon was closing at a steady 50 m.p.h. At two hundred yards out, Bolan sighed and gave the command. "Fire one," he said, the voice icy even in his own ears.

April banged the knee and replied, "One away," as the hot sizzler leapt away from the roofmount and rustled on ahead toward the target, the optics acquiring the fire instantly and bathing the command deck in the red glow from the viewscreen.

Dumb Visage lifted above the resting shotgun and just poised there, frozen, pondering the imponderable of a situation for which the fingertips had not been prepared.

And then it all went to hell, enveloped in flames and disintegrating within the firestorm, blowing up and out and all around the flat landscape as though a tornado from hell had reached up to reclaim its own.

"Bingo," April sighed.

The warwagon did not slacken pace but blew on through the burning debris as to the left and to the right the quick bodycount was read and evaluated.

"Three down, my side," April reported quietly. "Nothing moving."

So five men had died back there, quickly and savagely, perhaps without even knowing why.

And that was only the beginning.

Bolan turned the big vehicle away from the road and into a cane field, cutting a large circle and poising for re-entry onto the blacktop before bringing it to a full halt.

"EVA," April said sadly.

Nothing else would do. Bolan began drawing on the combat rig as he told his lady, "Fall back to the other side of the bridge. I saw a nice stand of trees about thirty yards east of the road. Take cover and get hard. Maintain radio contact with Grimaldi. Show no lights. Monitor my EVA channel but don't call me, I'll call you, unless it's a bonafide emergency. If I need some fire, I'll send for it. By the coordinates."

She replied, very quietly, "Okay. Don't worry about this end. Just watch your own."

He smiled, said, "It's always in sight," kissed her lightly on the lips, and bailed out of there for a doublequick advance with his brother, the night.

A mile of cane lay between the present position and the residence compound. He was carrying seventy pounds of warfare on his back and another thirty or so on the rigging. The night was settling firmly into place. And the Doomed

149

One Hundred, he hoped, were out there in that settling blackness awaiting the signal that would begin life anew. He hoped, yeah . . . he could only hope.

Jesus Christ the Goddamned son of a bitching no good bastard that pulled this shitface on Carlo the Pip should have his balls roasted over an open fire while they're still dangling from his bleeding body and Carlo by God would spit on that son of a bitch and whack those blistering balls with a ping pong paddle while the bastard screamed and begged for merciful death but there would be no Goddamned mercy for that rotten shit not while Carlo the Pip had anything to say about it!

"You got all those goddam people deployed like I told you?" he screamed at his yard boss.

"Yessir, just like you said, every man is up and on his feet."

"I want those feet *moving!* And those eyes, too! You keep them goddam eyes on the double stare and I mean it!"

Something went *ba-loom* in the night, faraway and dull, like distant thunder on a summer's evening. Rocky Vesperanza came sliding around the corner and bounded onto the porch, eyes rolling "Did you hear that?" he yelled.

"Hey I'm standing right on top of you, don't yell!" Papriello yelled, himself. " 'Course I heard it!"

"Came from the north side," the Rock said nervously, lowering the voice. "I just sent Johnny Bugs over there a few minutes ago to cover the bridge. I wonder . . ."

"Stop wondering and get 'im on the radio! Find out what that was!"

Vesperanza swiveled about and formed a megaphone with his hands to shout into the yard, "Try the radio, Harley! Ask Johnny what that was!" Then, to Papriello, "Are we sure about this? Are we real sure?"

The stupid question merely lathered Carlo the Pip all the more. "Whattaya mean are we sure! The rotten no good son of a bitch waltzed in here and . . . whattaya mean are we *sure*! Ask Mr. Santelli if he's sure he didn't send nobody, you dummyfucker! You go ask 'im!"

"I didn't mean—I mean—Jesus, I liked that guy, Pip, I mean I really liked him!"

"Aw naw, all you saw was his goddam broad!"

"Naw, but I mean maybe he was sent by somebody else, you know. Maybe Mr. Santelli wasn't supposed to know. Wouldn't we feel dumb if all Johnny Bugs turns back over there is a couple of busloads of broads?"

"Aw for my good grievin' mother's grave!" Papriello replied disgustedly. "That's all you're worried about, isn't it, your hot'n ready goddam broads. I swear, Rock, I never saw no guy would lose his head over a piece of tail the way you do! Do you know what poor Johnny Bugs may really be trying to turn back, over there? Do you know? Can you think of anything but spreaded legs?"

"If Frankie was a cop, Pip, then he's like no cop I ever—"

"Jesus Christ I don't believe it!" Papriello yelled. "Alla you boys out there, listen to this, I can't believe it! The guy I pers'nally hand-picked to be my number one cock has got nothing but his balls in his hand and snatch on his brain! He thinks our fancy friendly Frankie the Fink was a goddam cop! A goddam *cop*! I can't believe this!"

"I didn't say, Carlo, that—"

"It hasn't sunk in *yet*, I can't believe it! He thinks Mack the blacksuit *Bolan* was a goddam *cop*!"

Vesperanza took a step backward and said, "Who?"

A voice from the hushed yard called up, "I can't raise Johnny on the radio, Rock."

"Then say a prayer!" Papriello called back loudly. "Friendly Frankie is back in town! And alla you boys better damn well get set for a party without no broads because that's exactly what we're in for!"

Exactly, right.

But, to tell the truth, Carlo the Pip had kind of liked the guy, himself.

18

CLOSE ENCOUNTERS

Mack the Blacksuit had found slow going through the cane fields, with all that firepower weighting his steps across the soft earth. By the time he drew within good view of the lighted compound, the night was at its darkest. In an hour, maybe sooner, the moon would be rising. Until that time, he would definitely have an advantage over the enemy forces, being virtually indistinguishable from other dark pockets of the night.

The first encounter came in the cane, some forty yards outside the compound. Someone was moving slowly and cautiously through the growth, pausing every few steps to stand stock-still for a moment before moving on. Bolan studied the audibles of those movements then set a bisecting course. It was his practice to neutralize as much as possible the turf along his backtrack; he did not like to leave enemy patrols at his back and did not customarily do so if there was some way to avoid it. So he was going for this one, carefully maneuvering along an intercepting path.

Suddenly they were in the close encounter, separated by perhaps two-arm's-lengths of no-man's-land and a row of cane, Bolan in a half-crouch and the other standing stiffly upright in one of those rhythmic freezes, more visible by virtue of lighter clothing and breathing just a touch too hard. Then the opponent stepped off again and Bolan made his move, lunging up from the rear with a nylon garrote looping silently overhead to bury itself in unresisting flesh.

It was a little guy, not much more than a hundred pounds on the hoof, the backside of the body slumping against Bolan and molding itself against him in strange contours of defeat. A tightfitting cap slid off the head, releasing golden hair in tumbling torrents.

It was not a guy!

Bolan flung the garrote clear and quickly lowered that soft flesh to the ground. He massaged the bruised throat and pumped the diaphragm a couple of times to encourage a flow of air through those traumatized tissues.

It was not a guy, no. It was Jean Kirkpatrick

Russell, scared eyes as large as saucers, gurgling and gasping in the struggle for air. He continued to work on her until she was breathing satisfactorily on her own. She had apparently not lost consciousness at any point during the ordeal and she seemed to understand the situation perfectly, maintaining all the quiet possible under the circumstances.

Bolan placed his lips close to her ear and whispered, "Okay now?"

She sat up, both hands at her throat, and nodded her head in positive response. "My fault," she croaked. "My own fault. Don't apologize."

"I thought we had a deal."

"I couldn't . . . just sit there." The voice was coming better, now, a good sign. "Thought maybe . . . okay, I'm stupid. Mack, that man is the most important thing in my life. I had to . . . and I heard an explosion, and . . ."

He understood, and told her so, then asked her, "How'd you get here?"

"Boat," she whispered. "I tied it in the grass offshore and waded in. They're patrolling out there, all around."

He said, "Yeah, I know."

"What's happening?"

"Exactly what I promised you would happen," he replied. "But I still can't promise any results. And all you're likely to do around here is screw it up. Think you can walk okay?"

"I'm fine, yes."

He gave her a compass bearing with his arm and told her, "That's the backtrack. You beat it out that way, quiet and quick. It will take you to within a few hundred yards of the land bridge. Go on to the other side and look for a signal. Will you do that?"

She jerked her head in a nod of acceptance and asked, "What kind of signal?"

Bolan activated the shoulder-pocket radio and placed his lips close to the built-in mike. "Base."

April Rose bounced right back, terse but clear. "Go."

"Sending you a lady. Watch for her. Give her a sign."

"Wilco."

He told Kirkpatrick, "She'll have you in sight all the way across that bridge. Keep your eyes peeled about thirty degrees east. She'll guide you in."

"Right."

"Don't screw it up, Jean. Get clear and leave it to me."

"Right, don't worry, I've had my lesson for the night."

She brushed his face with hers and moved away, quiet and quick.

Bolan knelt in the dirt for a couple more minutes, listening in on his brother, the night, and thinking-in his strategy for the next move. Sixty pounds of explosives were in the backpack along with an assortment of timers and fuses.

156

The problem of the moment was to cover the final forty yards of canefield, breach the wire fence, and penetrate the defenses of that lighted compound to set his charges without any hue or cry.

It was not exactly a new situation for Mack Bolan. But this time, he knew, he did not have the element of surprise working for him. By this time, he was sure, Carlo the Pip would be up and ready for another visit by the Executioner. The guy was not a dummy, even though Bolan may have made him look like one. He was not a dummy, no. He was a capable and competent survivor in the most hazardous jungleland ever devised by the mind of man. And Carlo the Pip would be waiting, somewhere in there, for Mack Bolan's head to fall into his waiting sack.

"I want your best two men, radio-equipped, on walking checks constantly. I mean constantly. The whole perimeter, all of it, everything. I want every boy out there pers'nally eyeballed and spoke to at least once every five minutes. If two men can't cover it, then use what you got to use, but cover it."

"Right, Carlo. That go for the hammock, too?"

"Naw. Enzio and his boys will cover that in the boats. I'm not worried about that. Nothing out there that guy wants and the territory is too tight. The percentage play is right here. He'll be coming after *us*, Rock. First, anyway. So, now, you know how he operates. He comes in like a damned shadow and lays all over you. So we go to . . ."

"You was at that, uh, in Jersey, wasn't you."

"Yeh. I been tryin' to forget it, ever since. But, listen, there might be an angle there. In Jersey, he went soft on old man Marinello. After he blew 'im in half, of course. But he let 'em take the old man out. The guy's got soft spots in his head, if you can just find 'em. I been thinking. It might build our percentages some if we bring Doc Anderson and his hardhats over here. You know what I mean."

"You mean like hostages."

"Not exactly hostages, naw. Say, in his eyes, they're probably in the same league with us. But . . . wait a minute, Rock. I think maybe you said the magic words, there. He sure went to a lot of trouble to—maybe it wasn't all shitface—you know, what I told you, all that bleeding crap about the prisoners. Scurvy, for God's sake. That college boy we got working the boats says the scurvy is nothing but vitamin deficiency. You can't catch it. I figured the guy was just shitfacing me but . . . maybe it was more than that. Maybe he's really got a soft spot there. Listen, you better get on the radio and tell Enzio I said he should hold off on them guys. We might need 'em. And you better hurry 'cause I believe he's right now getting ready to load them in the boats and haul them off to the gator pond."

"Right. Should I also send some more boys over to the bridge?"

"Naw, I told you, that's too late. I bet the guy is looking at us right now."

Vesperanza turned his fat head and peered into the darkness beyond the lights, shivered slightly, said, "Don't say things like that," and trotted off on his errands.

Papriello snagged another lieutenant who was hurrying across the front yard, and asked him, "What about the monorail?"

"Jimmy Wheels is still working on it. Says the controls have been tampered with and he's trying to find where."

"You should give 'im a lawnmower," Papriello growled disgustedly. "Where you going?"

"I was going down to the dock to talk to Rudy."

"Rudy's doing fine. You stay here with me. I might need a runner and I don't want to have to depend on any of these green boys around here for something important. Even the Rock is starting to talk in whispers. Funny how that damn Bolan guy can get into your nerves, isn't it?"

"Well, Carlo, they all *saw* the guy walking around here today. And that's something to see. I mean, how many of us ever actually *saw* the guy? I mean in broad daylight." The yardman patted his chopper. "I'd just like to see 'im again."

Carlo the Pip shivered involuntarily.

The lieutenant chuckled nervously and said, "It's a little cool out here, tonight."

The Pip growled, "Yeah."

Two of the floodlights on the east side winked out suddenly.

Papriello softly exclaimed. "Watch it!"

"Maybe a fuse," said the lieutenant.

"And maybe not. Go see. And get those lights back on."

"Right."

The yard lieutenant hurried away. Papriello folded his arms across his chest and leaned against the porch railing, peering into the darkness at where the lights went out.

Something at the dark corner of the house quivered, or maybe his eyes quivered, Pip didn't know. A chill trickled along his spine as he strained to focus upon the darkness.

The guy had a way of getting into the nerves, yeah.

Papriello picked up his shotgun and trudged casually toward that darkened corner, feeling a little silly about the whole thing.

There was nothing there, either, but the Pip's overactive imagination—but a boy came running in from the eastside at just that minute with his breath all jerking around in his throat.

"What's the matter?" Papriello asked the kid.

"We found a cut in the fence. And Jerry C-Note laying in the cane with a choker buried around his neck."

"What? Where?"

The kid pointed into the darkened quadrant. "Right over there. I swear I passed that point no more'n two minutes ago, Mr. Papriello, and it was okay then. And Jerry's still warm."

The yard lieutenant hurried into that hushed conference with another breathless report. "The fuses are okay," he said. "But about ten feet of wire is missing."

Papriello's spine was doing its little dance, again. Something was lying on the ground beside his foot, something alien, something that really did not belong there. He knelt to pick it up and stayed there, examining it under his flashlight."

"Whattaya got?" asked the lieutenant.

"Any of our boys been picking sugar cane lately? Anybody even been *out* there?"

The kid said, "I was, sir. But that didn't come offa me. I wasn't standing there."

No, Papriello really had not even considered the possibility that one of his own boys had dropped it. And his spine had not been guessing at anything.

The son of a bitch had been standing there—in the darkness at the corner, with armed boys walking all around—just standing there, the nervy bastard, standing there in the dark and looking at Carlo the Pip.

"I'm going inside," he said casually. "Get that wire fixed and get those lights back on quick as you can. I gotta call Miami."

Yeh, dammit, he would have to call Miami,

now. With crap all over his face. With Guido missing and with Frankie the Fox for damn sure back in town. There was no quieting it, now, though he'd been hoping against hope that he could pull this thing out of the fire before having to report it to Miami.

How nice it would have been if he could have taken them Mack Bolan's head as the final item in that report. But "Frankie" was evidently foxier than Carlo the Pip had cared to remember. And it was no time, now, to be standing on dumb pride.

But, shit, the damned phone was dead, too.

The guy was laying all over them, all right.

Nothing ever really changed, did it?

Papriello turned out all the lights, released the safety on his shotgun, and sat down in Guido's chair. So okay. Let the bastard come. It was going to be every man for himself, anyway.

So let the bastard come.

19

THE DOOMED, THE DAMNED

The thing had gone without a hitch, so far. He'd found all the right avenues and created a few, here and there, of his own, and he had that camp wired to go on a ten-minute fuse. He left it, then, abandoning the empty backpack in the shack at the portal and quietly descending into the tunnel of love.

A guy down there in bluejeans and a greasy undershirt was sitting in the monorail car, puffing on a cigarette and staring with deep concentration at the control panel. He looked up and did a double-take on the imposing figure in black then quickly raised both hands above his head and yelled, "Okay, okay, I'm clean."

Bolan growled, "Haul the tail out of there, guy."

The guy began hauling it out, lowering one hand to haul with then bringing it up quickly, hauling hardware instead of tail. He did not even get it clear of the siderail. The silent Beretta spat once, sneezing out nine millimeters of sighing death and flinging tail and all clear of the car to fall bloodied-face down in the shallow flow of water beneath the car.

Bolan stepped over the body and into the car, popped the connector into place, and set sail for devil's island. There was no strategy beyond this point. He was strictly on the ear, now, hopefully prepared for whatever he may find over there and ready to take whatever advantage may present itself.

The activities in the dry hole appeared to have reached a more normal level—at least, a quieter one. The compressors were evidently shut down and the sounds coming from the lower levels were within tolerable range.

Two guys wearing bellbottom whites and toting automatic weapons were leaning over the guardrail, quietly watching the proceedings below. One of them looked around and reacted immediately as Bolan stepped clear of the monorail. The Beretta phutted twice again, closing the twenty-foot separation before either guy could bring his piece to bear on the problem. One of the hits was sloppy, though, tearing away a piece of cheek instead of reaming headbone as it should have done. That one's chopper went sailing over the side as he instinctively raised both hands to the damaged area. Another quiet round, following quickly, corrected the error and set things straight—but the falling weapon struck something solid down below and hit with a clatter.

By the time Bolan had stepped to the railing for a look-see, everyone down there was taking a look-see upstairs. Five hardhats were down there in clear view, grouped around a strange-looking vehicle which was suspended by a harness from the overhead crane. The thing looked a little bit like a submarine, a little like a military tank, and a whole lot like something from a science fiction movie. But there was very little opportunity for Bolan to make a detailed study of the strange craft. One of the hardhats jerked a pistol from his belt and started banging away at Bolan.

He stepped clear and went around to the control booth. Doc Anderson was in there, oblivious to the ruckus outside his soundproofed domain. Bolan went on inside, spun the guy around, and introduced the muzzle of the Beretta to his wide-open mouth.

"In phrases short and simple," he demanded coldly, "what is this you've got here?"

The man was nobody's fool. He knew exactly where he was at and what was going down. The lips made a couple of flaps without sound then found the way toward an intelligent response. "I have here, young man, the greatest natural wonder of the world."

"So why'd you sell it out?" Bolan inquired icily. "To the meanest perverts of the natural world?"

The guy bristled and said, "I tried all the others, first. I gave them all a chance. All the government agencies, all the foundations, all the academies. They laughed at me. They all laughed at me. Well. I found someone who didn't laugh. And with more resources than all the damned foundations combined."

"You didn't sell them a hole in the ground, Doctor. You sold them your soul."

"It's all one and the same thing," the guy said, with a shrug. "So it's okay. Go ahead and shoot me. I'll die a happy man, at least. I proved my thesis. Dammit, I proved it."

"I'm not going to shoot you, Happy," Bolan told him. He stepped over to the control panel and began studying it.

"What are you doing there?"

"I'm going to *dis*-prove it, guy."

"The hell you are!" The man came at him like a maniac, all rolling eyes and slavering mouth, grunting and panting and obviously determined to kill with his bare hands.

Bolan popped him once between the eyes with the butt of the Beretta, staggering the guy and setting him down. Then he grabbed him by the back of his collar and dragged him onto the catwalk, went back inside, closed and locked the door. While out there, he noted that the cable from the overhead crane was paying out. Those guys down below were apparently going ahead with whatever they'd been doing.

So was Bolan. It was a relatively simple control panel. Switches for "Inflow" and "Outflow," air pressure and water pressure gauges, level control readings. The only thing that really interested Bolan at the moment was the flow switches. He closed all the outflow and opened all the inflow—then, as an afterthought, opened a switch marked "Backflow to Lagoon." As a final item, he opened the panel door and dropped a grenade in there.

He was back on the catwalk beside Doc Anderson when the grenade exploded. But he felt rather than heard it. Even without the sound-proofed walls, Bolan doubted that he would have been able to hear such a puny sound, buried as it were in the deafening roar from below.

Fantastic columns of water were spouting into that once dry hole from six different levels along the sheer rock walls, as a gargantuan steel door slid aside to permit the unrestricted flow. And that hole was filling fast. The strange craft was bobbing around in that and Bolan could see two of the hardhats clinging to it for dear life as the torrents pounded at them. There was no evidence of the other three.

Bolan mumbled his regrets and walked out of there, leaving Doc Anderson gripping the railing like a man going down with a sinking ship and staring at the catastrophe with eyes already dead.

He surfaced with a sliver of golden moon edging above the flat horizon—and with quite a local disturbance breaking across the surface of the lagoon.

Several swamp buggies were jockeying around out there, caught in the sudden flow from an upgushing subterranean river and fighting to keep the awkward boats from being bowled over and swept away in the onrushing current.

The Doomed One Hundred were over there, as well, standing two by two in a double column along the water's edge. A ripple effect of excitement was moving along that column, produced perhaps by the "sign" in the lagoon. But that was not exactly the sign promised. Several bare-chested peers had broken the formation and were striding along the column, waving the arms and obviously trying to calm the promised ones. A couple of nervous guards with chatter-guns were trying to divide their attention between the phenomenon in the lagoon and the disturbed prisoners.

Well, Bolan had promised them a sign. But this one was coming straight from the ear. He unslung the M-16 combo, thumbed in a forty-millimeter round of high explosive, and let it fly toward the watch tower—then immediately repeated with another round flying toward the lagoon.

Two men came tumbling down from the flame-wreathed tower, the screaming descent partially eclipsed by the second explosion at head level among the struggling water craft.

That double column down there dissolved immediately, with people flowing joyously in every direction—some, even, into the turbulent waters of the lagoon.

Two more guys in fancy bellbottom whites came out of the trees by the lagoon and began spraying Bolan's general area with automatic weapons fire. But he could see a hell of a lot better than they could, moonrise or no; the answering burst from the chattering M-16 swept those two into a heap and rolled them back into the trees.

A ragged cheer went up from a group of nearby exprisoners—and it was at just that moment that the timed charges across the way found the end of their fuses. The residence compound at Santelli Island *whoofed* into the night with columns of fire and spinning fragments cutting donuts in the darkness high overhead. A voice in the distance behind Bolan screamed something unintelligible in a terrorized voice—and Bolan knew, by that single sound, that he'd broken the devil's back on this turf.

Water was beginning to flow from the portal, now, and was spreading rapidly along the decline to the lagoon. Two swamp buggies were overturned and showing their undersides while others raced in crazy patterns toward the outer waters.

Some of those among the formerly Doomed One Hundred were evidently getting into the spirit of liberation. Fires were breaking out along the line of huts. Sporadic gunfire also marked that moment and it seemed at least a reasonable assumption that the former prisoners were arming themselves with the abandoned weapons of their jailers. The assumption was quickly borne out, a moment later, when flames from the residence hall illuminated the tower area to reveal a disheveled smart-mouth turn-key frantically climbing that tower with two angry men in hot pursuit.

And then Bill Kessler walked up, hand extended and grinning from ear to ear. Bolan took that hand, and clasped it, saying, "Congratulations. You pulled it off."

"Like hell I did," said the liberated cop. "They were getting ready to feed us to the gators. We all know who pulled it off."

Bolan muttered, "Someone else sure wants to know." He turned toward the shoulder and hit the button to say, "Base . . . tell the lady her man is alive and well."

April's voice returned immediately, slightly perplexed. "The lady didn't show. Are those your fireworks?"

He replied, "Yeah. It's about over. Tell Alice

to send the barges. And ask Flyboy to come in on my channel."

"Roger, wilco. Hurry home. The second edge is restless."

"Soon," Bolan promised, and turned a concerned face to Kessler.

"Who were you talking to?" the guy wanted to know.

"Never mind," Bolan told him. "It's bad news. Jean Russell is roaming around here somewhere, on her own. I intercepted her over on the big island and sent her to the rear. She didn't get there.'"

Kessler groaned, and whatever he may have said with that despairing sound was lost in the crackling from Bolan's left shoulder.

"Flypaper to Striker. God, I see your tracks, guy."

"What's your position?"

"Directly overhead, at just about service ceiling. Five or six boats are streaming south in fast retreat. Any plans for those guys?"

Bolan replied, "Alice is waiting for them. Let him worry it. How's the visibility up there?"

"Moon's coming up, getting better all the time. What do you need?"

"A lost sheep. In a boat, maybe. Can you see anything that might fit?"

A moment later: "I see what could be a small swamp buggy fighting the current downstream from the lagoon. It's uh, wait, I'll get my night

171

glasses." Then: "Does this lost sheep have long blonde hair?"

Bolan said, "Bingo. Thanks, Jack." He turned to Kessler but the guy was already bounding down the slope and running like hell toward the open water.

Out there somewhere in the moonlight was going to be a joyous reunion.

And that was great with Bolan. Something along that line awaited him, too, he hoped.

He grinned and punched his shoulder button, again. "Come and get me, Jack," he requested, suddenly tired as hell. "Thursday is over."

20

EPILOGUE

Someone was banging on the door with a persistent rhythm and April was murmuring, "Oh, no, for God's sake, no—Mack, make them go away."

He clinched a towel to his waist, lit a cigarette, and went to the door.

Brognola stood just outside on the cargo deck of the Starlifter, hat in hand, apologetic smile on the tired face.

Bolan sighed and said, "Come on in, Hal."

The fed replied, "No, I don't, uh, want to intrude on anything. I see you're all buttoned down for the night. I guess we'll be lifting off pretty soon. Other vehicles are just about all

173

loaded. But I, uh, thought you may sleep better with an update."

Bolan told him, "I'd much rather take it sitting down, Hal. Come on in. We'll make some coffee."

"No, no. I'll just be a sec. They finally got the water shut off."

"That's good. Guess I excessed it a bit, there."

"No real harm done. Actually the 'glades were getting a bit dry in that region. They needed it. What I really came to tell you . . . Interior Department has put a seal on Satan's Hammock and a couple of bureaus are sending experts down for a full evaluation. So . . . who can say? It may turn out to be another world wonder or else the stickiest security problem we've had in years. It'll take a while to sort it out. Meanwhile your friend Kessler has filled in a lot of blank spots. He's a good cop, kept his eyes and ears open the whole while. Your guess was pretty well on target. They were lining up the entire American market for illegal narcotics. I've got, uh, some input from Lyons on that. Tell you about it tomorrow. But that was just for starters, probably. God knows what it would have eventually led to. But narcotics alone would have made the investment worthwhile. We're talking about a fifty-billion-dollar-a-year industry. Couldn't exactly call that a cottage industry, could you."

"Not quite, no. Come on in, Hal."

"No, that's all. Get your rest, you earned it.

174

Oh . . . also . . . the divers recovered eight bodies from that hole. Two were dead from gunshot wounds, the others apparently drowned. Anderson was among them."

"Uh huh."

"Yeah. Thought you might want to know that."

"Okay, thanks."

"Oh—and, uh, Grimaldi has come over, officially. We figured it's better that way. He may have been dangerously compromised during this operation."

"Glad to hear that. Jack will make you an excellent hand. I've been worried about his security, myself."

"We convinced him that he should start worrying, too. We don't know how many people managed to escape the big island. And, of course . . ."

"What was the bodycount?"

"Twenty-eight. And it could go up. But less than a dozen have been positively identified."

"Papriello?"

"Nothing positive, no. Several bodies were dug out of the ruins of the main house. But, uh, they were still trying to put the pieces together, last I heard. I'll, uh, try to get a complete report for your, uh, files."

Bolan sighed and said, "Okay, thanks. Either come in or say goodnight, Hal."

"I'm leaving. Oh—did April tell you? Santelli and his bunch were back on the street thirty minutes after we booked them. They're under surveillance, though. Right now they're on a flight to Washington."

"We'll worry that one tomorrow," Bolan told him. "Goodnight, Hal."

"Goodnight. Hey. What the hell you think I been standing out here jawing for? Don't you have something to tell me? Maybe I could rest better, too."

Bolan grinned. "Like what?"

"Like what the hell happens on Sunday."

"Didn't April tell you? I made that decision when I was seven years old."

"What?"

"Sorry. Private joke. Don't worry it. I'll be in Wonderland on Sunday."

Brognola huffed a sigh of relief. "That's wonderful. Okay. Go back to bed, dammit. And get some rest while you're there. We've got a tough one coming up tomorrow."

The chief fed spun on his heels and walked away.

Bolan closed the door, flung his towel toward the command deck, and rejoined his lady.

Thursday was over, yeah. But Thursday's heat was still going strong. "Now, where were we?" April purred, snuggling to him.

Nowhere. They were nowhere. And, at a moment like this, it was the only place to be.

Tomorrow would take care of tomorrow.

An insider's view of the *Death Merchant*— A master of disguise, deception, and destruction . . . and his job is death.

DEATH MERCHANT
by Joseph Rosenberger

One of Pinnacle's best-selling action series is the Death Merchant, *which tells the story of an unusual man who is a master of disguise and an expert in exotic and unusual firearms: Richard Camellion. Dedicated to eliminating injustice from the world, whether on a personal, national, or international level, possessed of a coldly logical mind, totally fearless, he has become over the years an unofficial, unrecognized, but absolutely essential arm of the CIA. He takes on the dirty jobs, the impossible missions, the operations that cannot be handled by the legal or extralegal forces of this or other sympathetic countries. He is a man without a face, without a single identifying characteristic. He is known as the master of the three Ds—Death, Destruction, and Disguise. He is, in fact and in theory, the Death Merchant.*

The conception of the "Death Merchant" did not involve any instant parthenogenesis, but a parentage whose partnership is more ancient than recorded history. The father of Richard Camellion was *Logic*. The mother, *Realism*.

Logic involved the realization that people who read fiction want to be entertained and that real-life truth is often stranger and more fantastic than the most imaginative kind of fiction. Realism embraced the truth that any human being, having both emotional and physical weaknesses, is prone to mistakes and can accomplish only so much in any given situation.

We are born into a world in which we find ourselves surrounded by physical objects. There seems to be still another—a subjective—world within us, capable of receiving and retaining impressions from the outside world. Each one is a world of its own, with a relation to space different from that of the other. Collectively, these impressions and how they are perceived on the *individual* level make each human being a distinct person, an entity with his own views and opinions, his own likes and dislikes, his own personal strengths and weaknesses.

As applied to the real world, this means that the average human is actually a complex personality, a bundle of traits that very often are in conflict with each other, traits that are both good and bad. In fiction this means that the writer must show his chief character to be "human," i.e., to give the hero a multiplicity of traits, some good, some bad.

At the same time, Logic demands that in action-adventure the hero cannot be a literal superman and achieve the impossible. Our hero cannot jump into a crowd of fifty villains and flatten them with his bare hands—even if he is the best karate expert in the world! Sheer weight of numbers would bring him to his knees.

Accordingly, the marriage between Logic and Realism had to be, out of necessity, a practical union, one that would have to live in two worlds: the world of actuality and the world of fiction. This partnership would have to take the best from these two worlds to conceive a lead character who, while incredible in his deeds, could have a counterpart in the very real world of the living.

Conception was achieved. The Death Merchant was

born in February of 1971, in the first book of the series, *Death Merchant.*

This genesis was not without the elements that would shape the future accomplishments of Richard J. Camellion. Just as a real human being is the product of his gene-ancestry and, to a certain extent, of his environment during his formative years, so the fictional Richard Camellion also has a history, although one will have to read the entire series to glean his background and training.

There are other continuities and constants within the general structure of the series. For example, it might seem that the Death Merchant tackles the absurd and the inconceivable. He doesn't. He succeeds in his missions because of his training and experience, with emphasis on the former—training in the arts and sciences, particularly in the various disciplines that deal not only with the physical violence and self-defense, but with the various tricks of how to stay alive—self-preservation!

There are many other cornerstones that form the foundation of the general story line:

●Richard Camellion abhors boredom, loves danger and adventure, and feels that he may as well derive a good income from these qualities. The fact that he often has to take a human life does not make him brutal and cruel.

●Richard Camellion works for money; he's a modern mercenary. Nevertheless, he is a man with moral convictions and deeply rooted loyalties. He will not take on any job if its success might harm the United States.

●The Death Merchant usually works for the CIA or some other U.S. government agency. The reason is very simple. Richard Camellion handles only the most dangerous projects and/or the biggest threats. In today's world the biggest battles involve the silent but very real war being waged beween the various intelligence communities of the world. This war is basically between freedom and tyranny, between Democracy and Communism.

(The Death Merchant has worked for non-government agencies, but he has seldom worked for individuals because few can pay his opening fee: $100,000. Usually, those individuals who could and would pay his fee, such as members of organized crime, couldn't buy his special talents for ten times that, cash in advance.)

•The Death Merchant is a pragmatic realist. He is not a hypocrite and readily admits that he works mainly for money. In his words, "While money doesn't bring happiness, if you have a lot of the green stuff you can be unhappy in maximum comfort." Yet he has been known to give his entire fee—one hundred grand—to charity!

•Richard Camellion *did not* originate the title "Death Merchant." He hates the title, considering it both silly and incongruous. But he can't deny it. He *does* deal in death. The nickname came about because of his deadly proficiency with firearms and other devices of the quick-kill. (All men die, and Camellion knows that it is only a question of *when*. He has never feared death, "Which is maybe one reason why I have lived as long as I have.")

•The weapons and equipment used in the series do exist. (Not only does the author strive for realism and authenticity, but technical advice is constantly being furnished by Lee E. Jurras, the noted ballistician and author.)

Another support of the general plot is that Camellion is a master of disguise and makeup, and a superb actor as well.

It can be said that Richard Camellion, the Death

Merchant, is the heart of the series; but *action*—fast-paced, violent, often bloody—is the life's blood that keeps the heart pumping. This is not merely a conceptual device of the author; it is based on realistic considerations. The real world *is* violent. Evil *does* exist. The world of adventure and of espionage is especially violent.

The Death Merchant of 1971 is not necessarily the same Death Merchant of 1978. In organizing the series, we did use various concepts in constructing the background and the character of Richard Camellion.

Have any of these concepts changed?

The only way to answer the question is to say that while these concepts are still there and have not changed as such, many of them have not matured and are still in the limbo of "adolescence." For example:

We have not elaborated on several phases of his early background, or given any reasons why Camellion decided to follow a life of danger. He loves danger? An oversimplification. Who first called him the Death Merchant? What kind of training did he have? At times he will murmur, *"Dominus Lucis vobiscum."* What do the words "The Lord of Life be with you" mean to Camellion?

All the answers, and more, will be found in future books in the series.

Camellion's role is obvious. He's the "good guy" fighting on the side of justice. He's a man of action who is very sure of himself in anything he undertakes; a ruthless, cold-blooded cynic who doesn't care if he lives or dies; an expert killing machine whose mind runs in only one groove: getting the job done. One thing is certain: he is not a Knight on a White Horse! He has all the flaws and faults that any human being can have.

Camellion is a firm believer in law, order, and justice, but he doesn't think twice about bending any law and, if necessary, breaking it. He's an individualist, honest in his beliefs, a nonconformist.

He also seems to be a health nut. He doesn't smoke, indulges very lightly in alcohol, is forever munching on "natural" snacks (raisins, nuts, etc.), and uses Yoga methods of breathing and exercise.

Richard Camellion is not the average champion/hero. He never makes a move unless the odds are on his side. He may *seem* reckless, but he isn't.

Richard Camellion wouldn't turn down a relationship with a woman, but he doesn't go out of his way to find one. The great love of his life is weapons, particularly his precious Auto Mags.

As a whole, readers' reactions are very favorable to the series. It is they who keep Richard Camellion alive and healthy.

The real father and mother of Richard Camellion is Joseph Rosenberger. A professional writer since the age of 21, when he sold an article, he worked at various jobs before turning to fulltime writing in 1961. Rosenberger is the author of almost 2,000 published short stories and articles and 150 books, both fiction and nonfiction, writing in his own name and several pseudonyms. He originated the first kung fu fiction books, under the name of "Lee Chang." Among other things, he has been a circus pitchman, an instructor in "Korean karate," a private detective, and a free-lance journalist.

Unlike the Death Merchant, the author is not interested in firearms, and does not like to travel. He is the father of a 23-year-old daughter, lives and writes in Buffalo Grove, Illinois, and is currently hard at work on the latest adventure of Richard Camellion, the Death Merchant.